Eternally Yours

LUCINDA BRANT BOOKS

—The Roxton Family Saga —
NOBLE SATYR
MIDNIGHT MARRIAGE
AUTUMN DUCHESS
DAIR DEVIL
PROUD MARY
SATYR'S SON
ETERNALLY YOURS
FOREVER REMAIN

— Salt Hendon Books —
SALT BRIDE
SALT REDUX

— Alec Halsey Mysteries —
DEADLY ENGAGEMENT
DEADLY AFFAIR
DEADLY PERIL
DEADLY KIN

Lucinda Brant is a *New York Times, USA Today,* and *Audible* bestselling author of award-winning Georgian historical romances and mysteries. Her books are renowned for wit, drama and a happily ever-after. She has a degree in history and political science from the Australian National University and a post-graduate degree in education from Bond University, where she was awarded the Frank Surman Medal.

Noble Satyr, Lucinda's first novel, was awarded the $10,000 Random House/Woman's Day Romantic Fiction Prize, and she has twice been a finalist for the Romance Writers' of Australia Romantic Book of the Year. All her novels have garnered multiple awards and become worldwide bestsellers.

Lucinda lives in the middle of a koala reserve, in a writing cave that is wall-to-wall books on all aspects of the Eighteenth Century, collected over 40 years—Heaven. She loves to hear from her readers (and she'll write back!).

lucindabrant@gmail.com
lucindabrant.com

ROXTON LETTERS VOLUME ONE
A COMPANION TO THE ROXTON FAMILY SAGA

Lucinda Brant

A Sprigleaf Book
Published by Sprigleaf Pty Ltd

Eternally Yours: Roxton Letters Volume One
Copyright © 2015, 2018 Lucinda Brant. All rights reserved
Editing: Martha Stites & Rob Van De Laak
Art, Design, and formatting: Sprigleaf

Sprigleaf triple-leaf design is a trademark belonging to Sprigleaf Pty Ltd.
Georgian couple silhouette is a trademark belonging to Lucinda Brant.

Typeset in Adobe Garamond Pro.

Also in ebook, audiobook, and other languages.

ISBN 978-1-925614-40-4

10 9 8 7 6 5 4 3 2 1 (i) I

for

my readers

CONTENTS

Foreword   xi
From the Editors   xvii

NOBLE SATYR LETTERS

1. Mlle Moran to M'sieur le Duc d'Roxton   3
2. The Earl of Strathsay to his Countess   7
3. Mlle Moran to M'sieur le Duc d'Roxton   11
4. Estée Montbrail to Mme de Chavigny   17
5. Mlle Moran to M'sieur le Duc d'Roxton   21
6. Mlle Moran to Signora Maria Casparti   29
7. The Duke of Roxton to his Duchess   35
   Renard's Poem to Antonia   39
8. Antonia's Father to his Mother-in-law   41
   Noble Satyr Family Tree   47

MIDNIGHT MARRIAGE LETTERS

1. Lady Vallentine to Lord Vallentine   51
2. Mr. Martin Ellicott to The Duke of Roxton   59
3. Mr. Martin Ellicott to The Duke of Roxton   71
4. Mme Vallentine to La Duchesse d'Roxton   77
5. Lord Alston to The Duke of Roxton   87
6. Sir Gerald Cavendish to The Duke of Roxton   91
7. La Duchesse d'Roxton to Mr. Martin Ellicott   95
8. Lord Alston to Mr. Martin Ellicott   101
   Midnight Marriage Family Tree   105

AUTUMN DUCHESS LETTERS

1. The Duke of Roxton to Lord Alston — 109
2. Roxton to Antonia—his last letter — 113
3. Antonia Roxton diary entry — 119
4. Deborah Roxton to Lady Mary Cavendish — 123
5. Mr. Christopher Bryce to The Duke of Roxton — 129
6. Mr. Charles Fitzstuart to Major Lord Fitzstuart — 135
7. Mr. Jonathon Strang Leven to Mrs. Charles Fitzstuart — 139
8. Antonia Roxton diary entry — 143
   Autumn Duchess Family Tree — 149

Behind-The-Scenes — 151

FOREWORD

By Her Grace, Alice-Victoria Edwina Hesham, 10ᵗʰ Duchess of Roxton, upon the sesquicentennial of the marriage of Antonia Moran to Renard Julian Hesham, 5ᵗʰ Duke of Roxton.

IT IS WITH IMMENSE pride and satisfaction that I offer this, the first of a two-volume companion set of letters—a selection of correspondence authored by my esteemed forebears, and persons important in their daily lives.

This first volume is published to coincide with the commemoration of the sesquicentennial of the marriage of my French ancestress Antonia Diane Moran, granddaughter of the Jacobite General James Fitzstuart, 1ˢᵗ Earl of Strathsay, to Renard Hesham, the 5ᵗʰ Duke of Roxton, my husband the present Duke's great-great-great-grandfather, and whose Christian name he proudly bears.

The compilation came about in the most surprising of circumstances, and it would be remiss of me not to mention what was reported in the newspapers, not only here in England, but across the Atlantic in New York City. No doubt the New York reports are because of the American branch of the Roxton family that has resided there since the founding of that great nation. The family's continued political influence in that democratic landscape today is represented most particularly by Senator Hubert Charles Fitzstuart, himself a direct descendant of the 1st Earl of Strathsay, of which we are immensely proud.

A few years ago at my family's seat in Hampshire—Treat —the vast collection of books and monographs housed in the Treat library were being re-cataloged and the library itself renovated, when workmen came across a secret door within the framework of the oak paneling. The existence of this door had been lost to family memory, and it is the opinion of experts that it had been sealed since the turn of this century, and well before Her Majesty ascended the throne. Subsequent research by Professor West-Hamilton of Trinity Hall, Oxford, the renowned expert on the Roxton genealogy, and author of the acclaimed biography of the family's great medical philanthropist Lord Henri-Antoine Hesham, younger son of Antonia Roxton, has revealed that this door was sealed on the orders of Frederick, the 7th Duke of Roxton. This is not the place for speculation, but Professor West-Hamilton is of the belief that the answer may lie in what was discovered locked behind this door.

Opened for the first time in a hundred years, the door revealed a staircase lined with bookshelves. The stairs lead to the apartment above the library, which had been used as the private apartments of the Dukes of Roxton for four generations, until the time of the seventh duke. It was Frederick who had these private apartments converted into bedchambers and a schoolroom for his six daughters. It is thought that during this conversion the stairwell was blocked at either entrance, and the stairwell's existence forgotten by future generations.

The discovery of a secret stairwell is in and of itself most satisfying, for it is known that the Dukes of Roxton were great bibliophiles, and perhaps none more so than my ancestress, the fifth duchess. Antonia, Duchess of Roxton and Kinross, not only had the distinction of being a celebrated beauty of her day, but was also a bluestocking. She was a great linguist, too, for she could read, write and converse not only in her native French but was just as fluent in English, Italian, Greek and Latin. Thus it was not surprising to the family that the 5th Duke and Duchess would seek a convenient and private method of accessing the contents of their library via a stair between their most intimate of rooms and the library.

But what is surprising, and most revelatory, is what was discovered housed on the shelves that lined this secret stairwell. It had always been assumed by the family—indeed my husband was told the story as a small boy by his grandfather Anthony, the eighth duke—that the private correspondence of the 5th Duke and Duchess was deemed too intimate in nature, and thus the decision was made to destroy most of it on the orders of his father Frederick. This destruction was considered necessary not only to preserve the illustrious family and ducal name of Roxton, but the privacy of the various correspondents.

I can now reveal for the first time that this correspondence was not destroyed at all, but merely locked away from prying eyes. For upon the bookshelves in the secret stairwell are hundreds, if not thousands, of pages of private correspondence, not only in letter form, but in diary entries. There are red leather boxes full of letters, notes, small tokens, and bound diaries in the 5th Duchess's hand. All the diary entries are in French, of course, while the letters by various correspondents are in French, Italian and

English. A proportion of this correspondence has indeed been deemed far too intimate in nature for publication, and it is the Duke's and my express wish that it remain locked away, never to be accessed by family or scholar alike. Yet, this does not detract from the excitement of the family at this discovery, for the bulk of the correspondence provides a unique opportunity to add to the family history, and opens up a window to a bygone era, when ladies wore gowns which were wider than they were tall, men dressed in embroidered satins and silks which rivaled those worn by any female of the day, and sedan chairs were more numerous than hansom cabs. It was a world before the American and French Revolutions, before industrialization and big cities, when persons great and small went about their daily life at a much gentler pace; this was the world inhabited by my ancestress, and the ancestress of my husband Renard, the 10th Duke of Roxton's great-great-great-grandmother, Antonia Moran.

It is fitting then that this selection of correspondence be published in the one hundred and fiftieth anniversary year of Renard, the 5th Duke of Roxton's marriage to his young bride, Antonia Moran, a direct descendant of His Majesty King Charles the Second, and who in her lifetime married not one duke, but two—one English, the other Scottish, and as a consequence is the ancestress of two premier dukedoms in the Kingdom which have unbroken male lines down to the present day.

It must be stated that this publication and its companion volume are published in a private capacity, and are not for public consumption. They are meant for the shelves of select persons with an academic interest in the Roxton lineage who wish to gain a deeper insight into the lives and motivations of my ancestors.

I wish to acknowledge the tireless efforts of the Treat Librarian, Sir Elliott Fortescue Bt. and his assistant, Mr.

Percival Mandrake, Professor Sir Marcus West-Hamilton, and the eminent French linguist M'sieur Auguste Martin, all of whom worked upon this volume for three years, and continue to work on the next, and without whom this correspondence would not have seen the light of day. This volume is dedicated to my loving husband, Renard.

Alice-Victoria Hesham
Her Grace the Most Noble Duchess of Roxton
March, 1896

FROM THE EDITORS

THE LETTERS AND DIARY ENTRIES in this first of two planned volumes follows a chronological order. The first chapter begins with correspondence from the early 1700s, before Antonia Moran's marriage, up until she becomes the 5th Duchess of Roxton. The second chapter begins with a birth and ends with a birth, and deals with correspondence between family members and favored family retainers during the marriage of the 5th Duke and Duchess. The third chapter was the most difficult, not only in the selection of letters to be included, but the distressing nature of the contents of the correspondence and diary entries, as it deals with Antonia Roxton's great sorrow suffered at the death of her first husband, the 5th Duke, and the subsequent distress of family members. It was not the intention of Her Grace or us as the compilers to distress the modern reader with such heart-breaking correspondence, indeed with any of the letters included here, but to shine a light on the strength and depth of feeling which made the marriage of the 5th Duke and Duchess legend, not only to members of their own family, but far beyond their wider circle of friends, and down through the ages to our present time.

All translations from the French, as well as the Italian, were meticulously carried out by M'sieur Auguste Martin, for which the editors are most grateful.

Sir Elliot Fortescue Bt., C.B.E.
Professor Sir Marcus West-Hamilton, G.C.M.G., O.B.E.
April, 1896

NOBLE SATYR LETTERS

NOBLE SATYR LETTER I

Mlle Moran, L'appartement du Prince au Château de Versailles, to M'sieur le Duc d'Roxton, Hotel Roxton, Rue St. Honoré, Paris.

[*Delivered at Versailles via a servant.*]

August, 1745

M'sieur le Duc de Roxton!

I am Antonia Moran, daughter of your cousin Lady Jane Fitzstuart, and the Chevalier Frederick Moran. We have yet to be formally introduced but I am also your kinswoman through a mutual ancestor, your grandfather Henry, 4th Duke of Roxton. He is my great-great grandfather. I am soon to lose the protection of my grandfather, General Lord Strathsay, because he is dying. Both my parents are dead. I am an orphan, and being underage I require the protection of a family member.

All this you already know, either because you do have an interest in the members and genealogy of your illustrious family, or because I made this known to you. This is the fourth such letter I have written and had delivered to your hand. Also, I think my father he wrote to you some time before his death, outlining his plans for me, and asking that you, as head of the family, watch over me.

M'sieur le Duc you have yet to give me the courtesy of a reply.

I am not purposely rude, but my situation grows dire with the passing of each day. Nor is it my place to tell you your duty to your relatives, particularly one who to you must seem to have sprung up like a mushroom, as if from nowhere. But as head of my family it falls to you to offer me sanctuary. If I had anywhere and anyone else to turn to, I would do so. I have many times observed you at Court, and it is by common report you do not suffer fools, nor do you seem particularly concerned about the immorality of some of your actions. None of that is of concern to me. What you do is your own affair, as you would rightly tell me to my face, were I given the opportunity to speak with you.

What I am trying to say is that I am not in the least worried that others may think you an unfit and improper person to be my guardian, as my grandfather has counseled, and some at Court believe. They tell me they know you better and warn me against you. But I do not believe you to be inherently malevolent, nor did my father think so. Though you are, pardon me for stating the obvious but I would ever be truthful with you, sadly indifferent to the familial responsibilities that come with your rank and wealth.

All I require of you is sanctuary until it can be arranged for me to travel to London and the grandmother I have yet to meet. I have an uncle there, too, my mother's brother, who may also wish to own me. So your duty and responsibilities would start and finish with transporting me safely to England. Is that so much to ask of one to whom I am connected by blood? I think not.

So you see, M'sieur le Duc, I would only be a small inconvenience and take up very little of your time and effort.

Please do me the courtesy of replying by hand, or seeking me out at Court, at your earliest convenience.

Your humble and obedient servant,
Antonia Moran

The Right Honorable Earl of Strathsay, L'appartement du Prince au Château de Versailles, France, to the Right Honorable Countess of Strathsay, Hanover Square, Westminster, London, England.

L'appartement du Prince au Château de Versailles
September, 1745

Madam,

Soon your greatest desire will be granted. I am dying, and my passing will not be long in coming. You will be made a widow, and be free of me at long last. I have the [*suppressed*]. I wish to God you were the [*suppressed*] who had given it to me so I could hate you all the more. But to hate you more than I already do is an impossibility. My priest tells me I must forgive you. That for me to enter the gates of Heaven I must forgive all those who have sinned against me. In that way, not only will my conscience be clear, but so too will my soul.

Ah, but you and I know I can never forgive you, in this life or the next, to the eternal damnation of my everlasting soul. I have prayed to God and sought forgiveness for this, and that He in His wisdom will show compassion and understand why I cannot.

You tricked me in to believing you would join me in France when there was no hope the rebellion would be a success, and yet you did not flee. Instead, you betrayed me to the English. And you have been an unfaithful wife almost from the very beginning of our infamous union. And how I loved you! I can forgive your infidelity because I had never been faithful to any woman, except you. And then, when you left my bed for another's—for the bed of your sister's husband no less—I saw no reason to continue my devotion. I asked at the time, and I have continued to ask that question: How could you lie with your brother-in-law and betray your sister's love? And from the reports of you I have received over the years, you continue to have carnal relations with your brother-in-law, in defiance of the Commandments and God's law.

But who am I to judge? I, the great sinner General, who has his royal sire's weakness for women. Did I not cavort with you upon your visit to Paris, and yet I hated you at the same time? I wished I could have resisted you, and yet, glad that I did not because that coupling has provided me with a son and heir, and, God willing, a future for my earldom.

I have never openly acknowledged our son (with the hellish name, all to spite me and irritate me, witch!) but privately he was always in my will, and in my heart. He is, when all is said and done, my flesh and blood, and my son. I just wish to God he was not yours!

Your behavior is abhorrent and unnatural and because you continue to share your brother-in-law's bed (and is he not your brother, according to Scripture?) I will never allow our granddaughter within your corruptive orbit. Not that

I believe Antonia to be capable of being corrupted. She knows her own mind and has already formed strong opinions. To listen to her without looking at her one would think it is a youth who argues with you, and not a rare beauty, who is in your image, though more beautiful than you'll ever be because she has an untainted heart. If only she had been born male!

Oh how I wish I could be a flea in your butler's wig when you do finally clap eyes on our granddaughter! You will be mortified to see reflected in her unblemished face what was once your face, though the prettier. But if I have my way, she will only ever meet you cold and eaten up by maggots, to lay flowers on her grandmother's grave, though she never knew you, because that is the sort of girl she is.

She is a joy, and I am fortunate to have known her before my death. She does her father's intelligence and her mother's blood credit, which I claim as all mine (not a drop is yours, as far as I am concerned).

I am to sign a marriage contract for her to become one day the Comtesse de Salvan, and with that ancient name and my wealth, she will be a shining light at the French Court, and God willing, revert to the true faith, if my will is carried out to the letter.

I tell you this in the hopes you will have a shred of maternal decency and keep your distance from her. I hope and pray you never meet.

While I have dominion over my granddaughter's future, I can have little over my own. In good conscience, and because my confessor judges that I do right by my legitimate offspring, I cannot deny our son Theophilus (God's breath, but that is a frightful name!) who will inherit the title once I am gone, and be Earl of Strathsay. All I can hope for is that he has many sons to wipe away the stigma of having you for an ancestress and me for a sire. For who will want to commemorate the memory of a disease-ridden papist General, who failed to restore his monarch to his throne, and his heartless adulteress wife, the [*suppressed*] of Ely?

I am tired, and my dear sweet Maria, my good-natured common-law wife who will inherit all that I do not leave to Antonia, waits to hold my hand, to mop my brow, and whisper lies to me about getting well. All these tasks you should have performed for me, Madam, had you been a true and devoted wife, and a half-decent human being, all of which you are not.

I leave you, and pray that we never meet again in any life, this one or the next.

James Strathsay

Mlle Moran, Hanover Square, Westminster, England, to M'sieur le Duc d'Roxton, Hotel Roxton, Rue St. Honoré, Paris, France.

Hanover Square, Westminster, England
October, 1745

Je espère que cette lettre vous trouve bien, Monseigneur!

I wanted to let you know as soon as possible that Ellicott and I have arrived safely in London, and without incident. Oh, that is not strictly true! There was an incident, but not while we were traveling.

Indeed, the entire journey from Paris was very well planned and executed, and not one mishap did we have. Ellicott was most solicitous in ensuring that every stage, every mile, every convenience of travel was pleasant and uneventful. Of course, I know I have you to thank for this ease of travel. Your large traveling carriage, pulled by six swift horses and escorted by a contingent of outriders, was stared at all along the way. Peasants in the fields looked up and watched as we trundled by in this black and gold painted magnificent conveyance; as did the people going about their daily lives in the villages we passed through. And wherever we stopped for refreshment, we attracted quite a crowd. Ellicott was quick to supervise the unpacking of the *nécessaire de voyage* so that our inn fare was served up on porcelain plates, crystal tumblers, and silver cutlery. I do not think I have ever eaten such plain food using such exquisite utensils. Then again, I do not remember eating at all. Though Gabrielle she tells me I did eat and drink, but food was of no consequence to me.

The crossing from Calais to Portsmouth was smooth, again thanks to your sloop, which took us across the Channel without any trouble, and there, waiting for us at the docks, was your English carriage with your English driver and footmen, ready to take us on to London.

I will not bore you with my feelings, or how much I miss you, or ask you again why you were so cold to me in the library that you were an entirely different being to the one you were in your private apartments. I wish you had had the good manners to at least wave me off, instead of departing immediately for *l'Majesty's* hunt. I have thought about your hateful words and your abrupt departure for many hours and my confusion still remains. Now I find I have made myself ill with thinking, and I do not want to think about it at all, and so I won't.

As to the incident that happened upon our arrival in London…

Oh! But first let me tell you my initial impression of London. This place it is so very noisy. Much more so than Paris. I think that is because adding to the cacophony of carriages, criers, beasts of burden being taken to market, and the usual hurly-burly, here there are a great deal of building works happening throughout the city, or as Ellicott corrected me, Westminster, which is apparently another city entirely. Oh, and before I forget, I was most surprised to hear Ellicott speak in English. Like you when you speak the English tongue, he sounds a very different person. But whereas your English voice it is cold and uncompromising, when Ellicott speaks it he sounds friendly. So much so that I have decided to call him Martin. He tells me in a most pleasant way that I cannot do so without your permission. But as it is his name it is for him to decide to allow me or not, and so I told him.

Martin is too loyal a creature to go against you, and I do not wish to distress him, so I will continue to call him Ellicott in public, but in private I will call him Martin. The name suits him.

But again I digress from the incident I wished to tell you about. You may have guessed it concerns my grand-mother. *Parbleu*, but I was very nervous about meeting her! I did not know what to expect, but what I did not expect was to meet a woman who looks much younger than her years, who has the most astonishing head of red hair and, most surprising of all, to find she and I are very alike in countenance and form. *Incroyable*! Yes! Even I see that we resemble one another. I was very pleased by this discovery, but she was not. She looked me up and down with a frown and said to her friend Lady Paget in English that she was not at all sure she liked what she saw—which was I! Can you believe a grandmother would say that to her only grandchild upon first meeting? I do not think she realized then that I understand the English tongue almost as well as my own French, and thus her criticism of me. Lady Paget she told my grandmother in no uncertain terms that such a comment was ill-mannered, and that to criticize my appearance was to criticize her own. My grandmother was offended by this and not happy to be rebuked, and like a spoiled child she pouted and flounced to the window to hide her embarrassment. She then tried to make amends by giving me a light kiss to each cheek and patting my hand in a perfunctory manner I did not like in the least.

Monseigneur, I have never met a more vain creature! She cannot pass a looking glass without peering into it! And her manner of dress is quite alarming in that her sizeable breasts almost fall out of her low-cut bodice, so that whenever a man walks into a room he cannot but stare at such magnificence spilling forth for his admiration. If she were not my grandmother I would take her for a harlot. But I think it is more vanity than venery.

So this incident of which I have still to tell you about occurred when one of her male admirers came to visit and we were sitting down to tea and biscuits. Do you drink tea, M'sieur le Duc? I do not like it at all! It tastes as I suspect dishwater must. In fact there is no taste and yet here it is drunk in the best salons. Lady Paget she tells me English people cannot get enough of tea, and that it is so highly prized that the black leaves are kept locked away in silver canisters that require a key to open. Can you believe it? If I live to be a hundred, I do not think I will become accustomed to drinking this insipid beverage from China.

So again this incident. I am sorry for delaying the telling, but I have so much to tell you that it is all dripping off the nib of my quill in no particular order because I do not want to forget one thing about my first few days here in London.

Sitting down to tea and biscuits with my grandmother and Lady Paget, we were interrupted by a gentleman wearing the most absurd pair of breeches I have ever seen. And that is saying a great deal, given some of the ensembles worn about the halls of Versailles! This gentleman's name is Percy Harcourt and he is Vallentine's cousin, though they look nothing alike. Monseigneur, you must believe me when I tell you he was wearing spotted breeches! Yes! Spots! Black spots. The material itself was a velvet and woven in such a way as to appear like the skin of a leopard. A leopard I tell you! And with these spotted breeches he wore bright yellow stockings and black shoes. His frock coat was yellow with black lacings, so that the ensemble, when taken as a whole, reminded me of a mythical creature—half man and half beast! I could not stop staring at him! Harcourt thought it was because his attire impressed me. He even confided that such breeches are all the rage in Naples. I did not know what to say. But I did not need to say anything because he ran on at the mouth so much that I thought he had forgotten to breathe and would soon pass out from lack of air!

Of course he stared at me, too, as if I had two heads, and then at my grandmother and back again to me, so I think he was unaware of my rudeness. I did my best to control my giggles, hiding my smile behind my fluttering fan.

But I do not think my grandmother was so much upset by M'sieur Harcourt's extraordinary attire as she was by his lack of attentiveness to her. He spent most of his time over his dish of tea engaging me in conversation, which, to be truthful, I found tedious. Not only because he would insist in conversing with me in French (his French it is very bad indeed) but that he punctuated almost every sentence with "Extraordinary!" and "Upon my word!" and "I am beyond speechless!" which of course he was not because he kept on talking.

In the end, my grandmother was so exasperated with him that she pushed aside her dish and saucer with some violence so that it slid across the lacquered tray and off the edge of the table and smashed on the floor. To which my grandmother jumped up off the sofa and blurted out "See what you have made me do!". But not at M'sieur Harcourt, but at me! Why?

I was so shocked, as was everyone else in the room, that I excused myself with a headache, which I never get, and retired to my apartment, just to have a moment's peace, and so she could regain her composure. Lady Paget scratched on my door to see if I was all right, but I told Gabrielle to tell her I was already asleep. A lie. But I truly did not want any company at that moment.

After all that I had been through, and the anticipation of meeting my grandmother, then to finally meet her, such was my disappointment in her that I wondered if I had followed the right course in coming to her. Perhaps I would have been better off staying with Maria and returning with her to Venice. But it is early days yet, and so I am inclined to allow my grandmother to recover her shock and discomfort at having me to stay.

The one good thing to come out of all this is that I am far away from the Comte de Salvan and D'Ambert's petulance. Tomorrow I am to meet my Uncle Theophilus, and I pray that he is not like grandmother at all. I will let you know the outcome of that meeting in another letter. This one I will now conclude, as Martin has promised to take it with him upon his return to Paris in two days' time. I will miss his company. How you are managing without him, he and I both agree cannot be at all well. Please do not tell him that I said so. He would be mortified. He is a most discreet and loyal servant and devoted to you.

I hope you will do me the favor of a reply to this letter, so that I may know you are well. Please give my love to Madame, and to Vallentine. I will write to them under a separate cover, and hopefully before Martin's departure, so he can deliver those letters, too.

Love,
Antonia

NOBLE SATYR LETTER 4

Estée, Madame de Montbrail, Hotel Roxton, Rue St. Honoré,
Paris, to Mme de Chavigny, Hôtel de Créquy-Gravier, Saint-
Germain-en-Laye.

Hotel Roxton, Rue St. Honoré,
November, 1745

Dear Tante Victoire, I trust you are now able to walk
about on your foot better than the last time I visited you,
using the walking stick I sent. As it has a pretty pink
porcelain handle and is of the finest burled walnut, I hope
you will see it as an accoutrement and not as a necessary
aid to illness or age. I am told that such walking sticks are
becoming all the rage in the most fashionable salons,
where the young ladies are just as likely to carry one as
they are a fan, so you too must use it, to be seen to be up
with the times!

Is Francois well? And Hubert? How are your little birds in
this colder weather? Did you move their cages closer to
the windows in the conservatory so they have warmth
during the day? I know you were worried about a gutter

high up on the turret which was dripping water right into the conservatory, and onto the Turkey rug underneath the cages. I hope that is no longer a worry for you.

Before I forget to mention it, I have enclosed the medicine I spoke to you about, the powder from London. It is called James's Powders, and there are all sorts of claims as to its abilities, from curing gout to the common cold. Lord Vallentine he recommended it and had some shipped over. Everyone in London, it seems, uses these powders. His lordship swears by it for the easing of headaches, and he is confident it will help ease the pain you continue to have in your poor foot. Why even Roxton agrees that these powders could be of use to you. So please, Tante, please put your silly ideas about the English aside this one time and take the powders for at least a week, as instructed on the packet. You cannot complain about the English unless you at least try their remedies, and then if they do not work, by all means complain.

Tante, I am worried about Roxton. My brother he does not say so, and he has never been demonstrative with his feelings or his thoughts, but I know he is not himself. Vallentine he agrees with me. It is the little things I detect that he thinks I do not see. His great abstraction. He spends most nights walking the chestnut grove with his hounds. I know this because the servants are up and lighting the flambeaux for him to walk about as if he is in daylight! The amount of wax he uses is staggering. But as it is a mere pebble of expense to him, why should I worry? It is not the expense of it, but this incessant walking about at night, out in the cold, and sometimes for over an hour.

If you can believe it, he now avoids the library, his favorite place in the house! Yes, it is true, I tell you. When he does go there, Vallentine says he does not sit in his favorite chair, but takes the one opposite, as if his favorite chair it is somehow already occupied! It is most strange and alarming. And he has taken to sitting in the drawing room with his book. This is most disconcerting to us, who have never had his company when he has his nose in a book! Vallentine tried to rally him by suggesting they play at backgammon, but Roxton he declined, making some lame excuse about wanting an early night to bed! You must believe me! It is all true. I almost fell off my chair to hear this excuse. I am sure you are as shocked by this as I am. My brother in bed before midnight? Unbelievable!

I truly fear for not only his health, but also for his sanity. I thought him ill and wanted to call the physician, but Vallentine he said a physician cannot cure what is wrong with my brother. To my great sorrow and alarm I believe he is right. There is only one cure, and it presses on my heart to think I was the one who was so against the match. That perhaps if I had approved, or tried harder to dissuade our cousin Salvan to give up his ridiculous notion of wanting to wed Antonia to his son, there might have been some hope of another outcome.

I am missing Antonia's presence just as much as my brother, I fear, for the rooms of this big house are now no longer filled with her laughter, her chatter, and her great teasing of Vallentine, which made us all laugh, even my betrothed. There was a lightness about the place, of it always being spring, when in fact it was autumn all along, and yet, we who were in her company never thought so. It is now as bleak and cold as the bleakest of winter days, inside and out.

Why is it that it takes separation and sadness to lift the blindfold and see what we should have seen all along? I am not only talking about her presence, but that before she came amongst us we were existing day to day, but we were certainly not living. It is true. And none more so than for my brother, whose very English and phlegmatic attitude to life had never bothered me in the past. Yet now

I see it bothers him, too, for he is no longer indifferent to life, no longer unconcerned and bored by it. Antonia opened his eyes to other possibilities, and now, tragically, he can no longer close those eyes and pretend not to see the world as she does. But without her here amongst us, to keep our spirits lifted, to tease and cajole us, it has caused my brother to sink deep into a vat of moroseness, and, oh, Tante, he is drowning!

I tell you what I have told no one but my priest at the confessional. I cannot wait to be married to Vallentine and be on our way to the Italian states for our honeymoon, if for no other reason than to escape my brother's depressing orbit. To spend more time than is necessary in his company is to soak up his great sadness, and that I can no longer suffer. It is selfish of me, but I cannot help it, and Lucian he agrees with me.

Why oh why did I not insist Antonia remain with us until the marriage ceremony it was over with? Then at least the time it would have been happy, and I would not have the pressing feeling of guilt mixed with anger, at Salvan for putting us all through this torment, and at my brother for falling in love with this girl—of all the females who have crossed his path! Why must it be one who is betrothed to another? Why must she also be in love with my brother? It is unfair on them, but it is also unfair on Lucian and me when I want everyone to be happy for us!

Please pray for us, and for my soul, for surely such selfish self-absorption has blackened it in His eyes, and that, too, is my fault!

Roxton sends his love, as does my darling betrothed.

Your loving niece,
Estée

Mlle Moran, Hanover Square, Westminster, England, to M'sieur le Duc d'Roxton, Hotel Roxton, Rue St. Honoré, Paris, France.

Hanover Square, Westminster, England, January, 1746

Joyeux Noël et bonne année, Monseigneur!

The Twelfth Night celebrations they have just ended, but I could not sleep, so decided to write and tell you all about them.

You, I am very sure, know all about the silliness of this season in England, though I am certain you did not partake of it, but sat back and observed it all through your glass with that look, half-incredulous half-disdainful, which annoys others no end, but which makes me giggle! For I know inside you are shaking with laughter to see what people they will lend themselves to with the excuse that everyone they are silly upon such occasions, and never more so than on Twelfth Night!

I am determined one day Vallentine he will play at Bullet Pudding with me. Do you know this particular Yuletide game? Perhaps you played it as a boy? No! Even then I think you would have abstained but enjoyed watching others make fools of themselves. I do not doubt that Vallentine he was one of your hapless victims. But I know there is no malice in you, and that Vallentine he would have enjoyed the game for its own sake.

Let me tell you all about it. You will enjoy hearing how silly it is, particularly when I tell you who participated at the Twelfth Night revelries at Grandmama's house. Yes indeed, we played these games in her drawing room. I insisted, for how else can I become a proper English-woman if I do not know all the English traditions? And so I argued this to Theo, who argued with Grandmamma, and was supported in his arguments by Lady Paget, Miss Harcourt and her brother Percy. Finally, Grandmamma threw up her hands in capitulation, saying we could do what we liked. I see your smile at this great manipulation of mine. But it was for the greater good, I assure you. For why should we all not join in the revelries of such an occasion? While you would not join in, you would never stop another from such enjoyment.

So this game of Bullet Pudding. Let me tell you about it.

Firstly, what is needed for the game itself is—A quantity of baking flour, a large silver platter, and a bullet. Such strange things to bring together. *Incroyable*, no? The platter it is put in the middle of the table, and the quantity of flour is piled high into the shape of a steep mountain on all sides, a volcano of sorts. There is skill involved in making the shape, and the flour is tightly compacted so it neither slides down nor collapses in on itself, but remains in this volcano shape. Atop this flour volcano is carefully placed the bullet, and in such a way that it does not sink immediately. This perfect little round ball of lead must remain at the apex until the game, it begins. The placing of this bullet requires a steady hand so that it does not immediately fall through the flour to the platter and is lost. Which means the game it is over before it begins!

Theo has the steadiest hand, so it was left to him to place the bullet without disturbing the pyramid of flour. He took his time and was very careful and slow. But he was too slow for Grandmamma, who would not stop complaining that he was taking too much time, and that perhaps one of the servants would be better at placing the bullet. I do not know how Theo he kept his temper, but he did. I suppose there were a great many people standing around the table eagerly waiting to play this game.

So the bullet it was put in place, and then the fun it truly began. Everyone who is playing the game is given a butter knife. Each person then takes a turn to carefully insert their knife into the mountain of flour, and then withdraw the knife just as carefully so as not to disturb the flour and thus disturb the bullet from the apex. Once everyone has had their turn, it all begins again. Of course we all became impatient and this makes us falter. Most of us are laughing at the others as the flour it begins to subside and the bullet it begins to sink!

And what do you think happens when the bullet it disappears into the flour? We abandon our knives and take it in turns to poke our noses and chin into the flour to find the bullet. Using our hands is forbidden. The only legitimate way permitted to extract the bullet is using our mouths.

Of course by this stage, there are fewer of us playing at Bullet Pudding. Charlotte for one would not dip her face into the flour, neither would Lady Paget. Theo, he too was not eager to do so, but I said I would be more than a little upset with him if he did not join in the game. After all, if M'sieur Harcourt was brave enough to stick his face in the flour to find the bullet, as was I, why not Theo? So that just left the three of us with the others withdrawing and watching on in astonishment, because, Monseigneur, I was as determined as anyone to find that bullet, regardless of the flour to my face or gown!

But let me tell you that laughing and flour do not mix! I was having such an enjoyable time that I could not stop giggling to see M'sieur Harcourt and Theo, their faces covered in flour with only their eyes blinking out at me! I realize I too must have presented the same ridiculous sight to them, for we were laughing so hard, that we were blowing the flour all over the table! And poor M'sieur Harcourt, he ended up having a coughing and sneezing fit because he breathed in some of the flour, and it went straight up his nose, and his eyes they would not stop watering. Soon his face it was covered not in flour but a strange dough as his tears mixed with the flour, causing it to clump. The sight was most hideous, and because it was hideous we Theo and I laughed even harder. And so the cycle of silliness it could not be broken!

Naturally, Grandmamma she was not pleased to see the game turn to the ridiculous, and tried to call a halt to it, when at that moment, Theo lifted his head up out of the flour with an almighty dramatic whoosh, and there, clamped between his grinning teeth, was the bullet!

Everyone applauded wildly, I suspect with relief, but most of the laughter was directed at Grandmamma, because when she stepped over to put a stop to our silliness it was at the same time as Theo he lifted his head, and the flour on his face shot out like a great white cloud when he breathed out, and covered Grandmamma from head to foot in flour!

So you see why I think Vallentine he must play at Bullet Pudding with me.

I will tell you about one other game before I conclude this letter and try and sleep, because it is now very late and my candle will soon gutter. I could light another but Grand-mamma she now has the maids counting my candles and reporting back to her, so that she can determine for how many hours I remain awake at night when I should be sleeping.

I would like to think she is doing such a thing because she is worried after my welfare, but I am not so naïve. She worries, that is true, but worries that I am still awake late at night when she is entertaining one of her lovers, and that I might hear the comings and goings from her room. These lovers, they do not stay the night, and so the footmen they must wait up to show these footlickers (not a nice word I heard Theo use for these men who visit his mother) the door when it is time for them to leave. One night there was a very loud noise on the stair outside my room, and I am sure it was one of these men tripping, possibly over their own feet, as he scurried off into the night.

But I will not write any more details of that, because I think I have already mentioned these nocturnal comings and goings in a previous letter, and to repeat it will bore you. But what I will repeat about these carnal encounters is that while my grandmamma and her lovers gain a temporary satisfaction for the body, her heart, I am very sure, remains dissatisfied, and her mind empty. I do not see the point in satisfying oneself physically without engaging the heart and the mind in such pleasurable activity. Only then can one truly be satisfied. These men are young enough to be her sons, and I am very sure they are not thinking with their brain at all, and certainly their hearts are left outside the door. But I cannot deny that these nocturnal trysts do make me miss you all the more, because I miss making love with you very much. But this feeling is all the more empty because my mind and my heart are even more bereft without you. I miss most lying wrapped in your arms in your big bed, half asleep and yet half awake, with all the covers and pillows around us and we two snuggled in, away from the world, away from everyone and everything. Just the two of us.

See, I have wet the ink with a tear, and you will think me a great baby for my sentimentality, but I cannot help it. It is the way I am and the way I feel.

I have dried my eyes now, and will continue for a little bit and then will sleep. Perhaps tomorrow I will wake and find that there is a letter from you waiting.

So this other game we played tonight, after we had cleaned ourselves of the flour—though not very success-fully because Theo and I were still finding amusement in our appearances an hour later. We must have been grin-ning at each other, because Grandmamma she wanted to know what the private joke was, and it did not matter that we told her there was none. She thought we were keeping something from her!

This other Yuletide game requires a bowl of brandy, some raisins and almonds, and flame to set the spirit on fire. The raisins and almonds are put into the bowl and then brandy poured in, just enough to cover them. The brandy is then set alight! Yes! So that there is a blue flame and the bowl glows! What stops the breath and heart is that the players are then required to dip their fingers through this flame to pick up as many of the fruit and nuts as they can before their flesh it burns. Each player takes a turn, and depending on how many almonds and raisins are scooped up at each turn, more are added, and so is brandy, and relit!

I assure you none of us had our fingers burned. And the gentlemen with lace at their wrists removed it or tucked it up so it would not catch on fire, as apparently this happened to a guest at another party, who caught his lace on fire and then ran around the room screaming. Theo says he was not even badly burned, but it was the shock of the thing.

I managed to scoop up five almonds and two raisins for my efforts. But I was giggling, which did not help. The greatest part of this game is watching the faces of the others as they dip their fingers through the flame, at first horrified and transfixed, then when they are not instantly burned they relax a little, which is the wrong thing to do because they become complacent, and that's when the flame it will burn, if you linger.

I must go now as I am very sleepy. In tomorrow's letter I will tell you all about the hanging of mistletoe and how if you walk under it, it is mandatory to kiss the person who is standing beside you (if they are of the opposite gender). I have decided that when we share a house one day and it is Christmas time, I will direct the servants to hang mistletoe in every doorway, which will give us an opportunity to kiss as we pass from room to room. Do not worry, I will make certain not to linger in doorways this Christmas…

I miss your company so very much, and more so, if that is possible, at this time of year with all the family gathered enjoying themselves hugely. It does not seem right to do so without you here with us.

All my love,
Antonia

Mlle Moran, Hanover Square, Westminster, England, to Signora Maria Giovanna Casparti, Fitzstuart Il Palazzo, San Marco, Venezia.

[*Translated from the Italian.*]

Hanover Square, Westminster, England
February, 1746

Gentile Signora, Please excuse that I do not write you a detailed letter about my stay here, or that this letter does not answer all the many questions you put to me, which I know you are owed. But in my present state I cannot think of anything but my predicament, which, when I confess all to you, you will think me very bad indeed. But I pray you, dearest Maria, will forgive me this, and much more besides.

Why do I write in such a dreadful scrawl? Because my heart it is breaking. I have had little sleep, so I ask that you excuse my handwriting and my poor Italian. Oh, how I wish this were all that you had to forgive! It is the least of my worries.

Maria, last night I went to the theater and who should come in at interval but M'sieur le Duc d'Roxton! Yes, I tell you, it was Monseigneur come home at last. And without a word spoken by anyone to me that this event was to occur. They—Grandmère, Theo, Lady Paget, Charlotte—they all conspired to keep his return a secret from me. Why? Why should they do such a thing unless perhaps he wanted it kept from me? But then again I ask myself why, as I have asked myself many times over the past few months why has he not answered one of my letters?

Oh, Maria, my head and my heart ache so. My eyes have no more tears to shed but I cannot harden my heart. I was so very happy to see him that I rushed up to him without a thought to where we were or who was with us, and blurted out how I had missed him. I expected him to at least acknowledge that he was pleased to see me. But he did not. He accused me in not so many words, but I saw the look in his eyes, of embarrassing him in a public place. I should have remembered that the nobleman known to the public is so very different from the gentleman I know in private.

Of course M'sieur le Duc d'Roxton would be displeased to be so set upon in such a manner in a public place, whereas were we in his bedchamber Renard would readily have scooped me up into his arms and spun with me about the room until we were both giddy and had to fall amongst the pillows to stop ourselves collapsing to the floor, and all the while laughing!

I convince myself that whatever happens from this day forward, I will always have the memory of those six wonderful days spent together, just the two of us alone in his apartments. I told you in an earlier letter how I gave myself to M'sieur le Duc and still I do not have one regret. Not one. Not even this morning as I write you this letter with my eyes all red and puffy from crying and still not knowing if he truly does love me as much as I love him.

But before I continue, please, you must believe me when I tell you he did not seduce me. I remember that was one of your questions to me. Did I truly orchestrate my own seduction? I tell you emphatically that I did! He would never have trespassed into my apartment. But I trespassed into his, at night, in my chemise, and with my hair down my back—how could he then resist me? Ha! There, writing it down in this way has made me giggle at my wickedness, and I feel a little better for it. Imagine me, an ignorant little fool of the ways of the bedchamber, seducing the greatest *roué* in all Paris! I also imagine that now M'sieur le Duc he has had the time to reflect upon it, he is startled to discover the reversal of our roles in the game of seduction. For surely a great rake should be the seducer, not the pretty *ingénue*? Perhaps his so great arrogance cannot abide that simple truth, and that is why last night he treated me with the cold contempt he usually reserves for others?

But I do not care who initiated our affair. All I care is that it happened! But I do not blame him or myself, and would not change a minute of that time. Even now, now that my life is about to change in the most shocking of ways.

My dearest Maria, just when you think I cannot shock you further, I will, I know it, when I tell you I am almost certain, though I want to deny it, *enceinte*.

I have told no one, though I suspect my maid Gabrielle she knows. But of course she must! You no doubt think me an even greater fool for allowing this to happen. But how could I not? How could I have anticipated such an outcome? Now you think me even more foolish. But to be honest, the last thing on my mind while making love was the possibility I would fall pregnant! Now that possibility is almost a surety I do not mind in the least.

If my condition does one thing, it will end the Comte de Salvan's plans to wed me to Etienne. Though I would not put it beyond my grandmother's scheming to use this to marry me off even more quickly to the Vicomte. That is why I must leave here before my condition it becomes apparent. And because I do not want to be a burden or an embarrassment to my family, or to M'sieur le Duc, particularly if he does not truly reciprocate my feelings.

That is why I hope you will agree to my plans to come to you, so that I may have my baby in Venice.

Will you have me, dearest Maria? I can think of no one else who will be sympathetic to my predicament, who will look after me, and when the time comes, care for my baby, too. For I mean to keep it, not give it away as I have heard happens to the children born out of wedlock to females from good families. Why should I give up a child of mine, who is of my flesh, and which was conceived in love; of that I am convinced! I have the means to give it a good life, if one without a father, so it will never suffer from lack of love and comfort, even if its opportunities will be limited by its lack of birthright...

Oh, Maria, I am so sad. I cannot help my feelings for him, and for this baby that is yet to be born. I know you think me a little fool, but I suppose that when one loves deeply, the fall into despair, if it ever comes, is great. I doubt my heart will recover. Though, for the sake of this new life, I am determined not to wallow in self-pity. All our choices have consequences of some sort and thus I must abide by these, and make the best of them.

Now I must not write another word. Gabrielle has been in to me twice as Charlotte is due here to take me away to her brother's house. I will send this from that house, not this one, as I suspect my letters are being read, or so Gabrielle suspects. I do not know for certain if that is so. I hope to have your reply within the month. In the meantime I will make plans for my departure.

Love and kisses,
Antonia

Renard, Duke of Roxton, to Antonia, Duchess of Roxton.

[*Left on Antonia's dressing table the morning after their wedding night.*]

Antonia, I love you. Three simple little words, and yet never uttered or inscribed in ink by me to another living soul, only to you. I will never love another as I love you. I will never cherish another as I cherish you. I will always love only you.

This is the happiest day of my life. For it is the first day of the rest of my life, with you. Not yesterday when we were married, with witnesses in attendance, up before parson and reciting what others have done before us and will do after us. Me nervous, and you serene and steadfast. I could not wait for the ceremony to be over with, and our guests to leave. Yesterday was still the getting there, but today, now, here, just the two of us, today I am your husband and you are my wife. It still leaves me dazed to write such words, for I truly believed I would never marry. And then into my life you stepped, or should I say twirled, in your whirlwind of silks and smiles...

You sleep peacefully in our bed, while I cannot sleep at all. I fear falling asleep and waking to find you gone, of finding myself alone. I am sure this apprehension will ease with every night we spend together as a married couple, until one night I will fall asleep with you in my arms, and wake to you still snuggled in my embrace, and think it the most natural state in all the world. But do not ever think for a moment I will take you or our marriage for granted. It is precious; henceforth I pledge to nurture our union for the rest of my days.

You told me that once we shared a bed you found you could no longer sleep without me. I can no longer live without you. For with you I am truly who I am meant to be. I wonder now if I have been walking about as one dead, or as a specter, with sight, hearing and touch, but without the ability to feel. It is as if I have floated through life without experiencing any of it. When did I become like this? How have I walked the halls of kings in such a paralyzed state: Eating without tasting, looking without seeing, touching without feeling. And all the time with a heart that was disdainful, and a soul that was wasted. Until you.

I have always considered my birthright a burden to be endured, and in the most arrogant of ways. I am well aware of my preeminent place in this world, and I own to being conceited and vain. I have often taken without a thought for the consequences to others, and without giving freely in return. I am by nature wary and reserved. All this you know and accept, and have never been in awe. Nor have you ever doubted my right to be as I am. You love me unconditionally, and for that alone I am blessed. You have given me a wondrous gift.

You have always been prepared to see the good in others, first and foremost, and only want the best for them. I marvel at how you find joy in living each day to the full. To look on you, to be with you, to experience life in your company, is to be complete.

For you alone I strive to be a better man; to live a better life; to know its joys and its pleasures; to never disappoint you; and never will I squander a single moment of the life that is left to me—with you.

With this letter I enclose some lines of verse, with apologies to the seventeenth century poetess for taking liberties with her poem.

You have my whole heart, my body, and my soul.

I am eternally yours,
Renard

Oft I've conjured thee to appear
By youth, by love, by all their powers,
Have searched and sought thee everywhere,
In silent groves, in lonely bowers:
On flowery beds where lovers wishing lie,
In sheltering woods where sighing maids
To their assigning shepherds hie,
And hide their blushes in the gloom of shades.
Yet there, even there, though youth assailed,
Where beauty prostrate lay and fortune wooed,
My heart, insensible, to neither bowed.

In courts I sought thee then, thy proper sphere,
But thou in crowds were stifled there,
Interest did all the loving business do,
Invite the lovers and maids too.
Thy mighty force through every part,
What god, or human power did thee create
In me, till now, unfacile heart?
Yes, yes, my love, I have found thee now;
And found to whom thou dost thy being owe,
'Tis thou the blushes dost impart,
'Tis thou that tremblest in my heart.

I faint, I die with pleasing pain,
My words intruding, sighing break
When e'er I touch thy beauteous form,
When e'er I gaze, when e'er I speak.
Thy conscious fire is mingled with my love,
As in the sanctified abodes
Forevermore…

Chevalier Frederick Moran, Moran Il Palazzo, San Marco, Venezia, to The Right Honorable Countess of Strathsay, Hanover Square, Westminster, London, England.

Moran Il Palazzo, San Marco, Venezia
February, 1743

Madam,

Undoubtedly a letter from your estranged son-in-law after an absence of communication of more than six years must come as does a bolt of lightning, unexpected and unwanted. Indeed, I have written to you upon only two previous occasions. I do not choose the word 'correspond' because I received nothing by way of a reply from you. And that came as no surprise to me.

Thus, I am not in expectation of a reply to this letter. I will merely assume you are in receipt of it and, as you possibly did with my previous letters, consigned my words to the flames in your grate. However, I am in no doubt you are reading this missive, for how could you not? You are a female of shallow mind and outlook, thus all letters must be read regardless of the feelings for the correspondent—curiosity compels you.

To the flames you may put my letters, but you will have my words on your conscience forevermore. Of that I have not a shred of doubt. But let me satisfy your curiosity as to why the husband of your daughter and the father of your only grandchild would bother to waste ink writing to you—you, Madam, who failed to provide an ounce of motherly affection or love for your daughter or mine.

I write as a courtesy, nothing more. For while you may not have the decency to acknowledge your own flesh and blood, honor forbids me falling into the gutter to join you.

I have it on authority your son is a decent man, and so it seems your two children received their sense of honor and depth of feeling from their father. If not for the fact my wife had your flaming red mane, and my daughter has inherited your exceptional physical beauty, I would have doubts you brought forth children via your birth canal, and not via a warming pan introduced into your bed!

I wrote to you on the joyous birth of our first and only child, a daughter, Antonia Diane. She was so wanted and her birth eagerly awaited. She has never disappointed. She is a blessing and has been a joy from the moment of her first cries. And what she has inherited in beauty she has ten times in intelligence, curiosity and compassion. Call it an eccentricity of my own intelligence, but I have always decried the stupidity of not allowing a superior intelligence to reach its full potential through study at our universities, regardless of family circumstance or gender. Antonia would have made an excellent scholar and no doubt followed in her father's footsteps and become a physician, had she been allowed to fulfill her intellectual potential. I have taught her as best I can, and employed tutors as if she were in fact my male heir, and she has exceeded my expectations. She can speak, read and write in Latin, Greek, French and Italian, as well as English. She is a voracious reader, and as inquisitive. And all this at just fifteen years old! I wish I had been granted more time on this earth to bear witness to her as a woman. But I digress upon a subject that is of no interest to you.

Did you, Madam, offer one ounce of praise or of welcome upon your granddaughter's birth? Did you even enquire after the welfare of your only daughter after a long and tedious labor? Not a drop of ink from your quill did you spare, heartless creature!

The only other time you have had the privilege of seeing my handwriting was to learn of your daughter's death in childbirth. My dear sweet Jane did her best to give me a son, only for her and the child to die in the attempt. I did not even have the consolation of holding my dead infant son in my arms. I wept for both, but most bitterly and long for the untimely demise of the love of my life at the tender age of only two-and-twenty. I have missed her every day since her passing. And my daughter has grown up without benefit of a mother's love and devotion. You would have seen my tears mingled with the ink in the letter I sent informing you of her death, and not one word of consolation, not one ounce of compassion, nor of understanding and shared grief could you spare us.

So why do I attempt to shake your conscience into action upon this occasion? Because, Madam, I am dying. I do not want or ask for your sympathy. I am in pain, yet I do not fear death. Death will release me from earthly feeling and reunite me with my wife and son. But I shall resist my demise with every fiber of my being until I am certain my daughter's future is secure. Antonia will be left an orphan, and I am certain it will be before her sixteenth birthday.

She will be alone in the world, but for her grandfather—your estranged husband, you, and your son—her uncle.

To Antonia you are all strangers, and because you are devoid of maternal feeling, Madam, she would be better off were I to consign her guardianship to the rag-and-bone man at the steps of our villa!

While I have every faith her grandfather would come to her aid, he is old and frail, and I am also told he will exit the world before I do. And thus I have reached out a hand to one who I know will do his duty as Head of his family, the family to which my daughter belongs, and take it upon himself to be executor of my last will and testament. I speak of His Grace the most Noble Duke of Roxton, your cousin.

And with the Duke as executor, I have made your son, Theophilus Fitzstuart, the 2nd Earl of Strathsay (for he will soon inherit the title), my daughter's guardian until her twenty-first birthday, whereupon she will inherit my considerable estate.

You must be wondering why I confide such mundane and, to you, unnecessary details. Because I forbid you to interfere in my daughter's future in any way. You have not made an attempt to enquire about her in my lifetime, so do not make an attempt to ingratiate yourself into her life once I am gone. I know you better than you think—if you thought there could be a way of using my daughter as a weapon against your estranged husband, you would do so.

Know this—I have written to his lordship and given your husband my full support should there be any dispute as regards my daughter's guardianship and her inheritance. Under no circumstances are you to involve yourself.

My one concession to you, call it a parting gift, is that I

have not poisoned my daughter's mind against you. She remains ignorant of your reprehensible behavior and I hope always will. I did this for her benefit, not yours, and permitted her to grow up with the fairytale that she was possessed of kind and loving grandparents and a loving uncle, all of whom care about her welfare—albeit from the distance of English shores. You possibly scoff at my stupidity, but make no mistake. I have every faith in my daughter's intelligence. Five minutes in your company, Madam, and she will undoubtedly form her own opinion of you that will faithfully mirror mine! She is no fool. You would do well to remember that, should you ever meet.

I know we shall never meet again. My conscience and my life are without blemish and thus I am destined for Heaven. I am very sure my eternity and yours are set for different paths.

Your ladyship's son-in-law,
Chevalier Frederick Moran

[*This eighth and supplementary letter is included here, at the end of the first set of letters, and not inserted chronologically, because it was not amongst the correspondence discovered in the secret stairwell at Treat, but was always in possession of the Earls of Strathsay. It was generously offered for copying and inclusion in this volume by the Lady Violet Fitzstuart, eldest daughter of the 8th Earl of Strathsay, and sister of the present (and 9th) Earl. It adds immeasurably to understanding the earlier years of Antonia Moran before her marriage to the 5th Duke of Roxton, when she resided in Venice with her father, the esteemed physician and Professor of medicine, the Chevalier Frederick Moran. The Chevalier wrote this letter just before he died of his final illness, which left his young daughter an orphan.*]

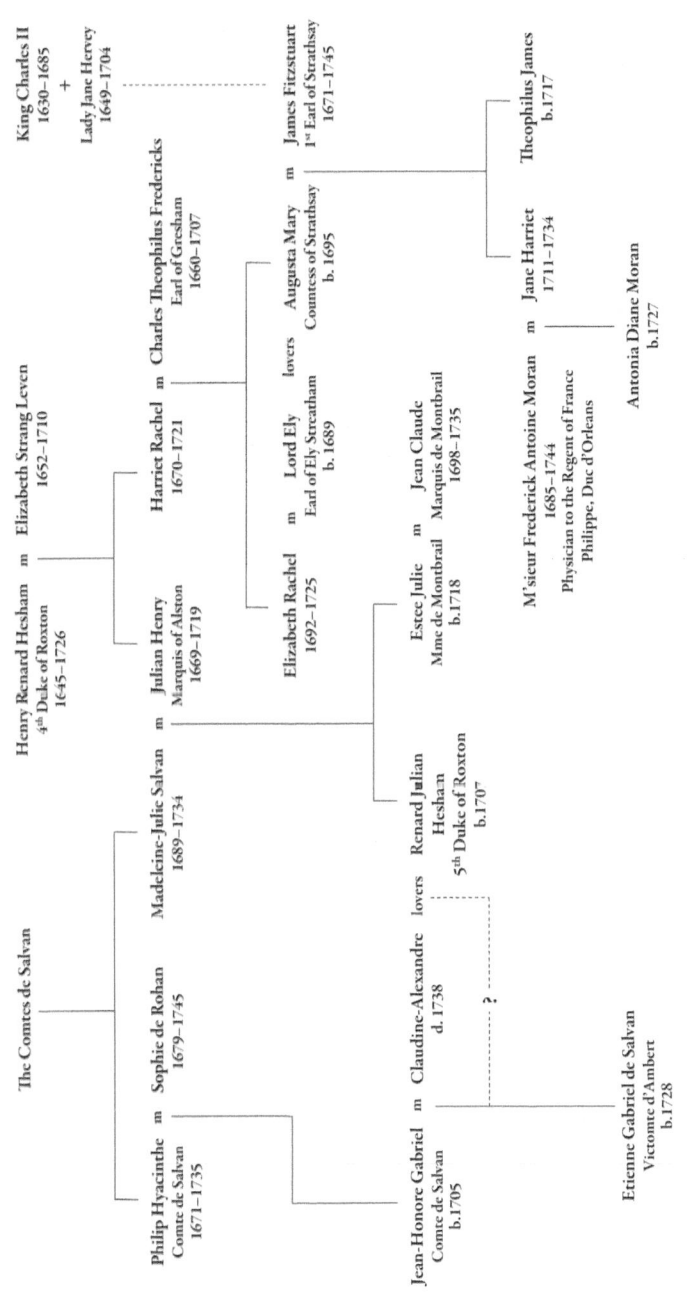

King Charles II
1630–1685
+
Lady Jane Hervey
1649–1704

Henry Renard Hesham m Elizabeth Strang Leven
4th Duke of Roxton   1652–1710
1645–1726

Charles Theophilus Fredericks m
Earl of Gresham
1660–1707

James Fitzstuart
1st Earl of Strathsay
1671–1745

The Comtes de Salvan

Philip Hyacinthe m Sophie de Rohan   Madeleine-Julie Salvan
Comte de Salvan   1679–1745   1689–1734
1671–1735

Julian Henry m
Marquis of Alston
1669–1719

Harriet Rachel
1670–1721

Augusta Mary
Countess of Strathsay
b. 1695

Theophilus James
b.1717

Elizabeth Rachel
1692–1725

Lord Ely   lovers
m Earl of Ely Streatham
b. 1689

Jane Harriet
1711–1734

m M'sieur Frederick Antoine Moran
1685–1744
Physician to the Regent of France
Philippe, Duc d'Orleans

Renard Julian
Hesham
5th Duke of Roxton
b.1707

Estee Julie m Jean Claude
Mme de Montbrail   Marquis de Montbrail
b.1718   1698–1735

Antonia Diane Moran
b.1727

Jean-Honore Gabriel m Claudine-Alexandre   lovers
Comte de Salvan   d. 1738
b.1705

?

Etienne Gabriel de Salvan
Victomte d'Ambert
b.1728

MIDNIGHT MARRIAGE
LETTERS

MIDNIGHT MARRIAGE Letter 1

Estée, Lady Vallentine, Hesham House, Hanover Square, London, to Lucian, Lord Vallentine, Ffolkes Abbey, Ely, Essex.

Hesham House, Hanover Square, London
August, 1761

Lucian, you must return to London at once! We need you
—Roxton needs you.

Something… something utterly shocking has happened. I can hardly bring myself to write. I have been shaking all over these past three hours, and only now have mastered the tremors and my tears, so that I can finally dip my quill in ink and scratch the parchment without dropping great blobs of black all over the page. In truth, this is my third attempt at writing to you, and if it were not for the courier kicking his heels in the courtyard, his horse saddled and waiting, he ready to ride posthaste to you, I would give up the attempt, and throw myself back on my couch.

But write I must, and tell you a little of what occurred so you will not worry on your return journey. But most importantly, so you will not come blustering in here, slamming doors and shouting, demanding all sorts of nonsense, not least of which that our son be thrashed for his part in an incident almost beyond imagining, that has left me, his dearest mamma, bereft of speech and not able to look at him without bursting into fresh tears for his part in this wickedness.

Of course I know they are but mere boys and were stupidly intoxicated, and that he and his friend Robert had no part in the shocking deed perpetrated late last night... But they did nothing—nothing—to stop it either, so my brother has every right to think them equally as guilty. So you must come and speak to these boys and find out the truth of the matter. Know that they have come to no harm, but are detained, under house arrest (the shame of it all!), on pain of punishment if they dare try to leave the house without first giving a full account of their actions, and what they witnessed, to M'sieur le Duc.

But my poor brother is in no fit state to interview them. Thus our dearest boy and his school friend will at least have some hours or days! to sleep off their drunkenness. I pray then they will be able to give a better account of themselves to you. But your first duty must be to Roxton. Evelyn you can interrogate later. And it would not do him a harm either for those boys to spend time alone with their thoughts and to think through their deplorable inaction.

No! I have not been drinking, or taking too many James's Powders. I grant I have not slept all night, and am exhausted from being in attendance on Antonia, but I cannot close my eyes, which are dry of tears because I see the nightmare of last night as vividly as if it were happening all over again. I screamed, I know I did. And it is my screams that still ring in my ears. That poor sweet darling girl did not so much as whimper until her pains they began. I believe she was in shock; is <u>still</u> in shock that such a monstrous act was perpetrated upon her, and in her condition! Oh, Lucian! She was so very brave!

And so you must return here with all haste, and not stop until you are in his house, and can help my brother with the unspeakable reality that his son and heir is a monster. A monster, I tell you! And others will attest to this sad fact, so I am not the only one who thinks so.

It is dawn and the morning sky is streaked red. That is not such a good omen, is it, to think the new little one's first day in this world will be full of storms, when this birth, so longed for and so anticipated, should have been joyous, wondrous, an event most worthy of the noble parents, and yet, it has turned into a catastrophe of a magnitude most shocking.

It is as if one son he has run mad and in his place is this puny but perfectly formed little bundle of bittersweet joy. For all that, he is very much alive, determined in fact, to remain on this earth and not ascend into Heaven. His cries are lusty and demanding and he has taken to the wet nurse's breast with gusto. So that must say something for his will to live and gives us hope that he will one day thrive.

Yes, Lucian, Antonia has given my brother a second son. But she is too weak to feed her infant. She is almost too weak to live. She has lost a great deal of blood, and her spirits they are so low that the physicians have advised Roxton that even if she manages to rally physically, her poor mental state may see her decline further. But we— Roxton and I, her maid Gabrielle, and those who love and know her best—put our faith in her strength of person-ality and great will to live. She would never willingly leave Roxton in this way, and she could never abandon her newborn son.

And so the new little one, as I told you, has been given to a wet nurse, a sturdy young wench who has no history of drinking or carousing, and has just the sort of disposition needed to care for a premature newborn of an ailing mother. She will stay by Antonia's side, despite the physician's advice the Duchess needs rest and no distraction. But Antonia wants to be near her newborn son, to see him for herself and hold him between feedings, even though she can barely hold up her head, and needs assistance to drink from a pap cup.

Roxton agrees the infant remain within the sickroom, and this despite the physician advising him in private that there is a chance his newborn son will not live out the week, and the devastating effect this will have on Antonia were she to witness him taking his last little breaths and then expiring in front her! Oh, Lucian, just the mere thought of such a horrendous circumstance, after all they have been through—the babies they have lost before this one—to have a second son and then to lose him within the blink of an eye, it makes my heart break.

I tell you, Lucian, my brother has aged ten years in ten hours! You will not know him I think. I am certain his hair is turning white before my eyes, and his eyes, they are full of such sadness. Forgive me the splotches. I did not think I had tears enough left to shed. But there you are!

Lucian, oh Lucian, what has become of us? Why has our world been turned upside down in this way? How could that boy do this to his mother? What demons are in his head? Between you and me, I cannot but help recall the incident with the Vicomte d'Ambert, wherein he attacked Antonia and almost killed her when she was pregnant with Alston. And now this! Sixteen years on and that infant in the womb turns around and does the very same thing to his own sweet mother? It is beyond belief! My brother must surely wonder what blood runs in his veins to have produced such monstrous offspring. But I will say no more about it, and you would do well to burn this letter before your return. My fears in that direction I pray nightly are wholly unfounded and some other explanation can be found, but what that could be, is beyond me!

I have not had the heart to broach the subject with Roxton, and with Antonia unable to rally after a most traumatic labor, he has not been a minute away from her side, not even to visit Alston, who remains locked up in his rooms, refused all contact with family or servant.

And can you blame my brother, when it was he who returned to the horrific sight of his dearest darling Antonia being dragged into the winter night air in her night attire, out into the square, by her son. Her son, Lucian! Not a fiend, or a criminal, or an escapee from Bedlam. But her most precious eldest son, whom she worships almost as much as she does her husband! Yes, it is true I tell you. Her son, my nephew, Alston dragged her from her rooms and down the stairs and out into the night! He cast her out of the house and into the streets, as if she were a whore not worth his spit. And that is what he said to her. Accusing her of being a bawd, and that the child she carried as being the bastard offspring of her lover. My God, can you believe he accused his mother of adultery? Antonia, of all women on this earth? She the beauty of her age who is so utterly devoted to my brother, a reformed satyr, that they have been the butt of many a ridiculous cartoon not fit to print—but print it they do! I tell you, Lucian, such disgusting drawings would never be printed in Paris! At least France has a secret police to protect us! But I am rambling, but who can blame me?

No one, not I, not the Duchess's physician, not the faithful family retainers, not even his godfather M'sieur Ellicott, who had come up to London to be present for the birth in a few weeks' time, could tell Alston any different about his mother. At first we were all too shocked by his behavior and his actions to speak. And then it was almost too late to save Antonia from his wrath, when he pulled her after him, down the stairs and out into the night air! And that darling girl did not utter a syllable against him. I think she too was so shocked she lost the facility of speech.

He was drunk, Lucian. He was so drunk and full of angry tear-filled rage that it would not have mattered what Antonia or the rest of us had said to him, because he was incapable of listening to anyone or anything. He was as one blind to his outrageous behavior, and blind to the fact his mother had gone into labor. He had her by the arm and was shaking her, calling her the most appalling names and demanding of her who was her lover and the father of her bastard, and in such a rage that we were truly fright-ened he meant to hit her! Just the thought of it makes me faint!

And then, as if from nowhere, Roxton he was there! My brother, just returned from White's, came out of the dark-ness. He strode up to his son with all the energy and strength of a man half his age, such was his rage, and I do not doubt fuelled with fear for Antonia. He saw and heard no one but the outrageous scene presented to his shocked gaze.

Thank God he is ever the cool-headed one in a crisis. He did the only thing left to him. The only thing none of the servants, not Antonia, not I, or his family would do. He grabbed his son by the scruff of the neck and pulled him off his mother. He then gave him such a backhanded slap that it knocked the boy off his feet! Stunned, he crumpled to the cobblestones. And it was only then that it came to him what he had done, and what he might have done, to his mother and her unborn child. And then Alston he let out such a howl it was as if a wounded animal had come amongst us.

Antonia she fell into M'sieur le Duc's arms. And within the blink of an eye, as only Roxton's presence can command, everyone was quiet and everything still. The chaos and the madness it was over with! My brother scooped Antonia up into his arms and marched indoors, leaving his son sprawled on the filthy cobbles, sobbing.

It was only then that our son he appeared out from the darkness, too, and with him his school friend Robert. They were sheepish but not afraid, and very drunk! Both boys were seized upon by Roxton's servants, and despite my protests, despite my tears, all three boys were taken away, marched from the square, and taken inside the house and locked up! It was left to Roxton's servants to clear the square of onlookers, and to Martin Ellicott to help me inside, and we followed my brother and Antonia back up to her rooms, where I have been ever since, except now, to write you this letter, to tell you to come home at once!

I cannot lie to you, and you must know for my brother's sake, that Antonia was close to death and her labor over with so quickly that there is still a small chance of her not recovering from her ordeal. Lucian, she may not return to us. Her infant he breathes and he suckles but he is so very small. I have lit candles and prayed and prayed.

I do not know what will happen to Alston, or to our son. All I do know is that we need you here, that my brother he needs you here. So for God's sake, get yourself a strong swift horse and ride like the storm which is fast approaching!

Your loving wife,
Estée

Mr. Martin Ellicott, Esq., Third Hill Residence, Constan-tinople, to His Grace The Most Noble Duke of Roxton, c/o William Kinloch CDA, His Britannic Majesty's Embassy, Athens, Greece.

Third Hill Residence, Constantinople
June, 1767

Dear M'sieur le Duc et Mme la Duchesse,

I trust this letter finds Your Graces, Lord Henri-Antoine, Dr. Bailey, and the various members of your travelling party, in excellent health, and enjoying the warmer weather the Mediterranean affords.

Julian and I were overjoyed to read in your most recent missive that you are now only a month away from us. Your imminent arrival reminded us that we have resided in this city for almost three years, when we had planned to stay a mere 12 months. But there is so much to see and do, as you will discover upon your visit, that even after three years we are still uncovering aspects of this city new to us. Not to mention the numerous overnight journeys into the surrounding countryside, by ass or by small boat along the coast, that have taken us to places and sights that are a feast for the senses that, had we been home, could only ever be conjured up in the imagination from readings of the Scriptures.

Before I begin, let me assure Mme la Duchesse that I have managed to secure her desire for a sizeable house close by, a mere ten-minute walk from our own residence. Your party of fifteen will easily be accommodated within its white-washed walls, and this with the complement of some twenty native servants who all have various tasks to do, and who reside within the mansion's complex of buildings. There is a Syrian native major domo, a M'sieur Anawi, who is fluent not only in several languages common to this part of the world, but his French and Italian are excellent, both being the prime tongues amongst the elite—local and foreign.

The house has an exceedingly pleasant aspect, with views of the surrounding hills and the harbor, and in the afternoon a refreshing sea breeze comes up the rise. All the rooms have cathedral ceilings with large picture windows, no glass, but shutters when needed, and are draped with oriental silks. The floors are marble, which is pleasant and cool underfoot in this warm climate. There is a scattering of sizeable oriental rugs. The ones in your private apartments are woven in brightly-colored silks and are indicative of the area. They were purchased, as you requested, to be taken up and shipped home upon your departure. I only hope that my taste in such furnishings is to your taste. But as you have assured me in the past that this is so, I will own to being proud of the selections I have made on your behalf, Mme la Duchesse.

The main part of the house is built around a large internal courtyard, open to the elements, that has at its center a rectangular bathing pool that is tiled with the most delightful mosaics and is entered at one end by a number of wide shallow steps leading down into the water. All the main public rooms open out onto this area, with its filtered sunlight, large pots containing palms, and numerous divans with their cushions, to sit and rest upon with guests, as is the way here. Or, as often happens, meals are taken in this area, with the bathing pool a welcome distraction before or after meals. Your private apartments also has a bathing pool, smaller in size but deeper. I hope you will approve and find that it is not inconsiderable.

The mansion is set in lush grounds which remind me of an oasis we visited in Syria, with date palms, vines, colorful flora, and a watering hole for the native birds. All of it is surrounded by a very high wall, higher than a man standing upon the shoulders of another. This will afford privacy and allow Lord Henri-Antoine to roam about without fear of him wandering off, though the number of servants would preclude this ever happening.

The property is leased for six months as was agreed, with the option to extend for a further six months, though I understand you desire to return to Paris for Christmastime.

One last matter regarding the house. I have had M'sieur Anawi allocate the rooms in the manner Your Grace specifically requested, and that one be set aside for Julian in the family wing so he may stay with you during your visit. I agree with you, that he should do so, if for no other reason than to make a connection with the little brother he has yet to meet, but as to whether he will, that is a matter requiring the greatest tact on your part, M'sieur le Duc, of which I know you are well aware.

But before I speak of Julian, let me say how gratified I am to read you enjoyed your stay in Rome, and that you were pleased with its relics, and more so with the treasures to be found at the Vatican. Of course who could refuse you a tour of those statues, paintings and treasures acquired by His Holiness's agents throughout Europe and beyond? That you were able to meet up with the Vallentines in Rome, and enjoy some weeks staying at their villa, must have made for a happy reunion, particularly after a separation of some months' duration. That M'sieur and Mme Vallentine have decided to return to Florence, and to the house of M'sieur's cousin, who is consul, I am not surprised. And to own to a truth, it is better for Julian that this family reunion is a more intimate affair, and conducted without the presence of the Vallentines, regardless that their son remains in Paris. More on that subject you may discuss with me at your leisure when you are here.

I was greatly encouraged by your report of Lord Henri-Antoine's health. That he has not suffered a bout of the falling sickness in over a month must surely bode well for his little lordship's future, and be such a relief to you both. I hesitate to suggest that as you travel south into warmer weather this has had a beneficial effect on his humors? He sounds such an inquisitive child, that perhaps he has been too distracted with not enough time to take ill on your travels?

I must tell you that Dr. Hakim is very desirous of conferring with Dr. Bailey, as he assures me there are treatments and medicinals in this part of the world which may alleviate his little lordship's symptoms, if not provide a cure. Dr. Hakim comes with the highest recommendation, and lest you think I go by recommendation alone, I had the physician call upon me and over a cup of Turkish coffee we spent a pleasant hour in discussion on all manner of subjects. I found him unassuming and interesting, and never boring. Mme la

Duchesse, I think you will find him a great conversationalist.

We are both so looking forward to meeting Lord Henri-Antoine. Can he be almost six years old? It seems only yesterday Julian was running around in breeches for the first time in Mme la Duchesse's garden at Treat. And to think my godson will be turning one-and-twenty while you are here, makes me shake my head at the passing of time!

Naturally, your visit is badly wanted. Your eldest son has missed you both extremely, as you well know from his letters and mine. If he is not immediately demonstrative of his true feelings upon this family reunion, it will only be because he wishes to appear a man, and thus, even with me and others, he does his utmost never to show his distress in public. As you can imagine, he still carries a great burden of guilt upon his young shoulders, and I fear always will, where the birth and health of his little brother are concerned. I have no wish to distress you or cause you to relive such a sensitive episode, but as I have been charged with your son's welfare, I think it important you know his state of mind.

This reunion has filled him with the greatest apprehension, not only because it will be the first meeting of the brothers, but even more so because he wonders how you will receive him. I know. I know. You will both welcome him with joyful open arms, but it does not matter that I tell him so. He must experience it for himself, and then I think his mind will be settled.

As you do not keep any secrets from each other, I write openly and always honestly. But as to the next topic, I have enclosed a separate sheet of parchment on the understanding that you may wish to burn this particular page, given its sensitive nature, and yet keep the rest of the letter

intact. I trust you will not think this gesture an imperti-
nent one, but one born of necessity. Thus I will continue
now on separate correspondence stock before returning
here to finish my missive.

[*Here is the aforementioned single sheet, on separate parchment (written both sides), now returned to its original letter.
It was not burned as was advised or predicted, but found
amongst M'sieur le Duc's most sensitive correspondence, in
one of several locked red leather portfolios found in the secret
stairwell within the Treat library.*]

M'sieur le Duc, to be brutally honest, your visit
here and our return to Paris with you cannot
come soon enough. While this delightful sojourn
in Constantinople has been one of our most
pleasant foreign stays, we have prolonged our
departure by a twelvemonth, and all because of
Julian's carnal association with a particular female
whose husband is attached to the Russian
Embassy.

I do believe had we made our plans just over a
year ago, Julian would have acquiesced without
question, and been glad of the change of scenery.
He was growing restless by that time, for us to
make the voyage by sea to Alexandria. We had
discussed visiting Cairo and then making another
sea voyage along the coast of Africa and on to
Gibraltar, and thence up the Channel to France,
to return to Paris.

These plans I had almost in place when they were
thwarted. Julian caught the eye of the wife of the

Russian *Chargé d'affaires*, one Prince Vladimir Rostovsky. The husband is frequently away from the city and to other parts of the empire, on business, leaving his childless wife behind, she preferring not to travel. She, too, is nobility, a princess of the Gargarins, and they both conduct themselves as if their umbilical cords are attached to the Empress herself. Meaning, they look down upon those who are not of equal status, and are as one blind to any menial below that of an Imperial lady-in-waiting. She expects all gentlemen to be in awe of her beauty, and he that every gentleman bow and scrape before him. In short, they are a well-matched couple.

The Princess Sonia Natalia Gargarin-Rostovskia is a willowy beauty, with pale skin, dark eyes and coal-black hair. She is eight, possibly ten, years Julian's senior, but looks younger. And so she should, because her time is spent almost exclusively in the upkeep of her person. And yet, for all her vanity, she is an accomplished linguist, and such are her abilities that she is often called upon by the embassy to sit in on meetings requiring an interpreter. I concede she is a gracious hostess and pleasant enough company, from what I have witnessed on the handful of occasions I was in her presence at an embassy function. But of course, it is not for her conversation that Julian seeks her out.

When the Princess first showed an interest in Julian, I was not surprised. As you will discover yourself, your son has grown into a handsome young man, tall, broad-shouldered, with a wide lean frame. He has a devastatingly handsome smile, has inherited Mme la Duchesse's extraordinary eyes, your deep smooth voice, M'sieur le Duc, and has a deference and natural noble bearing about his person, all of which combine to make him irresistible to females.

What surprised me was that he would be interested in this female, and that she would continue to hold his interest. Until the Princess, Julian has shown only polite curiosity in the opposite sex, and never expressed the desire or need for sexual congress with any woman, despite the many overtures he has received over the years, from females of the highest rank to those paid for their services, from Dover to Rome, and now here in this city. Thus it is not through lack of opportunity but a natural reticence, and dare I say an innate prudishness, which has kept him chaste. That is, until now.

As she is a married lady, and one who is discreet, I was inclined to look upon their affair, for that is what it is, as no bad thing. After all, with her he has received the best sort of introduction to the pleasures of the flesh, without the attendant worry of scandal had she been younger, fertile, and less accomplished.

But their affair recently took a dangerous turn when the Princess's husband walked in on his wife entertaining Julian. For while Rostovsky was aware of his wife's indiscretions, to find her on her knees for a vigorous male some fifteen years his junior was a severe shock to his manly pride. It has caused a public rift in their marriage, and he has demanded she break off her association with Julian. This she has refused to do.

Her refusal and subsequent behavior has led her

husband to throw caution to the winds and air this very private of matters in public. One evening, while drunk at the Occidental Club, and when I happened to be in the reading room after dinner and thus within his hearing, Rostovsky crudely announced that his wife had the most talented tongue in the Ottoman Empire. Of course this double entendre shocked those present by the very manner of its delivery rather than the revelation itself. I believe most members were unsure to what Rostovsky alluded, knowing his wife to be a renowned linguist.

However, the Prince could not leave it there, and continued to strut about the room pontificating. Firstly, that the duel fought between Lord Braithwaite and the Count Montessori, which had caused a sensation when Braithwaite was mortally wounded, was fought over the Princess. Secondly, that his wife was a cradle robber. Up until this drunken outburst, Julian had not been linked with the Princess, and there had been no public declaration on the part of her cuckolded husband as to his wife's infidelity. Yet this outrageous outburst followed up with the crude quip that his wife's young lover was a nobleman who was not only known to be a handful, but had given his wife quite a mouthful as well. He did not go so far as to state Julian's name publicly but I fear that is unimportant now. Particularly as Julian fails to see the seriousness of the rapidly deteriorating situation between the husband and wife, and continues to visit the Princess.

When I suggested Julian distance himself from her out of respect for her husband, his natural reaction was to tell me his affairs were not my concern. To which I replied it was very much my business, given I am acting *in loco parentis*, and what would his esteemed parents think of such a connection. He then became angry and told me there was no need for me to worry, for he knew what was due his name and had refrained from taking their trysts to their natural conclusion, and had no intention of doing so. That was his wife's prerogative only.

You will agree that this is a relief, though I am startled at such self-control and maturity, given his age and this his first sexual encounter. Yet, knowing his nature I should have had an inkling he remains a virgin from choice.

One would have thought that because he refuses to take their liaison to its natural conclusion, the Princess would break off the affair. She has no shortage of suitors, and her husband's rants have not deterred them—far from it, particularly with his crude advertisement as to his wife's talents. Yet, it seems the only male sharing her couch is your son, and every night, since her husband has taken to sleeping at the Club. She is ever assiduous.

I pondered this and believe I have arrived at a suitable explanation, one that will allow you to deal with the dilemma in your usual omnipotent way upon arrival here. For you see I believe the Princess, who is highly desirable and highly sexed, and used to getting her own way in all things, particularly where men are concerned, finds Julian's self-restraint a most potent aphrodisiac. And being a determined creature, she will not give him up until she has broken down his defenses. For in her mind, how can there be a man who can resist her considerable charms and expert talents?

I do not know to what lengths she will go to break his resolve, but as his desire for her shows no signs of abating, I believe her capable of anything to see herself the victor in this bedchamber melodrama. Make no mistake, M'sieur le Duc, the Princess Sonia is very intelligent, cunning, and determined, and if in the end she realizes Julian will not break (and I believe he will maintain his resolve, for he is assuredly mindful of his destiny, which should please you), then she is likely to turn on him in any number of ways to have her revenge on what she perceives as an attack on her self-esteem.

[End of single sheet of parchment.]

I have taken the liberty of drawing up a list of places you must visit while here, and Julian has been over the list and made a few recommendations of his own, one being a visit to the coast to the Palace of the Seven Towers. He has also added a number of coffee houses to the list, which he is certain his father will enjoy, there being one in particular which is solely given over to the sipping of the Turkish brew—called the wine of Islam, for they do not partake of alcohol—and the playing of backgammon. Julian is of the opinion that M'sieur le Duc will trounce all comers, and has the opportunity to defeat the reigning champion, one Pasha Bedri Ekrem, a retired officer who in his fifteen years of competition at this coffee house has never been beaten in the best of five.

I only wish Mme la Duchesse could witness such a scene, but alas, women are forbidden such places where males congregate. Not unlike the clubs in St. James's Street in London, though that is behind closed doors, whereas here, it would be the same as if every street in Westminster that housed a club or coffeehouse were forbidden women.

I cannot tell you how very much I am looking forward to the lively debate regarding this and many other topics upon your arrival, Mme la Duchesse.

I will sign my fist now so that this missive can be sent and reach you in a timely manner.

Your most humble and devoted servant,
Martin Ellicott

Martin Ellicott, Esq., Moran House, Bath Road, Avon, England, to His Grace The Most Noble Duke of Roxton, Treat via Alston, Hampshire.

Moran House, Bath Road, Avon, England
September, 1768

My Dear Duke,

This is in reply to your letter, enclosing Sir Gerald's recommendations, and seeking my opinion not only on those recommendations, but on the matter as a whole, for which I offer my advice.

The untimely death of your daughter-in-law's elderly chaperone, Miss Clementine Francis, some three months ago, was in and of itself a sad affair. Miss Cavendish (for I have always called her so and cannot defer to her married title until such time as she knows it herself) had grown genuinely fond of her distant cousin and was distressed at the old woman's passing. You would have been proud of how she, a young woman not quite twenty years of age, conducted herself. From the funeral arrangements to the little gathering after the ceremony, Miss Cavendish handled it all with a poise and maturity beyond her years.

And it is because of her conduct, and as one who has

studied her temperament first hand, that I believe what Sir Gerald suggests is entirely the wrong approach to take with your daughter-in-law. Particularly at this most sensitive time, when Julian has shown an interest in fulfilling his destiny and becoming a husband in more than name only.

Miss Francis was the ideal chaperone for a girl of Miss Cavendish's disposition. The old woman never presumed to judge her young charge, and entered into her plans for the future with her nephew as if these plans could be brought to fruition, though she knew in truth the reality was quite different. And although Miss Francis spent most of her time in a sunny corner knitting or reading her Bible, her eyes and ears were always open to signs of restlessness or distress in her charge. Dare I admit that her sedentary nature and mild-mannered demeanor were part of her appeal, for she never said a cross word and even when the house was at its most chaotic, as it surely must be with a determined young woman in charge of an active school boy, the old woman carried on as if she were housed in a nunnery.

As you are aware, Sir Gerald never approved of Miss Francis as a suitable chaperone for his sister, only seeing her in the most cursory manner. I am aware that Sir Gerald was of the opinion that what was required, after Miss Cavendish absconded to Paris to look after Otto, was a female of taciturn temperament and noble bearing, of whom the Bath Society matrons would approve.

If I may be blunt, Your Grace, the latter was all Sir Gerald truly cared about, and still does. The welfare of his sister is secondary to his wish that she not be talked about by Society. That she defied him and ran away from home almost brought on a nervous collapse in him, not because of his fears for his sister's safety, but because he feared your wrath in allowing it to happen.

I know it does not bother Your Grace in the least what Society thinks; your private affairs are no gentleman's business but yours. But I do know you care that your daughter-in-law remains a virgin for the consummation of her marriage to your son, and that since her return to England from France, scandal not attach itself to her name.

The butler Saunders continues to send me weekly reports of his young mistress's comings and goings, and the general atmosphere within her household. It has become apparent through these reports that your daughter-in-law has begun receiving visits from several suitors, and one in particular that I know will displease you greatly—Mr. Robert Thesiger.

I was not so concerned about these would-be suitors, or Mr. Thesiger's visits either, while Miss Francis was alive to keep a wary eye on proceedings. And lest you misconstrue me, I was never concerned how Miss Cavendish would conduct herself in the company of these young men, with or without Miss Francis present.

Your daughter-in-law may be headstrong and a tomboy, but she is modest in manner and deed, and has too much pride for her illustrious name of Cavendish and in herself, to consider a fall from grace. If I may be so bold to make a prediction, Miss Cavendish will make a most excellent Marchioness of Alston, a wife Julian will be proud of, and a daughter-in-law in whom you can safely charge the future of the Roxton dukedom.

But lest these suitors become bold, and I see Mr. Thesiger as being determined in his suit, I suggest that Your Grace see to it that Julian makes himself known to his wife at the earliest opportunity. How this is to be done, and how he conducts himself, is not for me to speculate or wonder at. My only part in this endeavor is to offer you my opinion, and to keep a protective eye on your daughter-in-law from the distance of my house on the outskirts of Bath.

In the interim, until such time as Julian arrives in Bath, I propose a novel approach to the replacement of Miss Francis, one that will surprise you and undoubtedly displease Sir Gerald, for it goes against everything Sir Gerald suggests. He would have Miss Francis replaced with a dour sour-faced jailer who has the manly strength to restrain his sister if called to it. In essence, Sir Gerald wants his sister kept prisoner until claimed.

I could not disagree more with this advice. Replacing Miss Francis with such a person will create great tension and disharmony within the Milsom Street household; it will become a most unhappy place, and one your daughter-in-law will wish to flee at the earliest opportunity.

Miss Cavendish is of a temperament that requires she feel she has some charge over her person and her house. To employ a female who would seek to restrain or take this from her would lead, I believe, to her taking a most rash action. She would again run away, and this time take her nephew Jack with her. I believe she is most likely to turn to M'sieur Evelyn Ffolkes, who offered his protection and name when she was last in Paris. A repeat of such behavior is the last thing you and your son could wish for, but that is my dire prediction.

Miss Francis never took it upon herself to accompany Miss Cavendish when she visited the Pump Room, nor was she inclined to be her shadow when she and her nephew strolled or rode through the township. And she never accompanied her on her weekly visits to me. Upon these excursions from the house, your daughter-in-law has been accompanied by Mr. Joseph Jones, her brother Otto's major domo, and since Otto's death, he has taken it upon himself to be protector to Deborah and her nephew Jack.

I would not be incorrect in assuming Joseph's presence within the Milsom Street household meets with your approval, and that at the very least he, too, has been charged with keeping an eye on Miss Cavendish, and more particularly, an eye out for any trouble that may be lurking near the vicinity of her person, such as the likes of Robert Thesiger.

Thus, I propose that Miss Francis not be replaced. Not having a chaperone in the short term will make no difference to Miss Cavendish's life, or change the opinions of those Bath matrons who live to spread spite about others. Bath's gossips may think your daughter-in-law is lacking a sensible adult eye upon her activities, but such a circumstance makes me smile smugly, for no young lady's actions, acquaintances and daily routine are more carefully scrutinized and monitored, albeit from afar, than that of your daughter-in-law!

Yes, having no female companion will set the Bath gossips to whispers and adverse remarks, but what is that to you in the grand scheme of things? What will it matter when Miss Cavendish becomes wife of the Marquis of Alston in more than name only, and she takes her place within the bosom of your family? What then the gossips and spiteful asides? They will be as nothing, and not one woman or man would dare make comment against her then.

I believe I have now exhausted the topic, and your time on the matter.

This letter is sent off without delay, and with my faithful assurances of replying to Mme la Duchesse's letter on the morrow.

Your most humble and devoted servant,
Martin Ellicott

Mme Vallentine, Hotel Roxton, Rue St. Honoré, Paris, France, to Mme la Duchesse d'Roxton, Treat via Alston, Hampshire, England.

Hotel Roxton, Rue St. Honoré, Paris, France
April, 1769

Dearest sister, when did you say you and my brother would be returning to Paris? I know you told me but I have misplaced that letter, and I am too fatigued with worry to go searching for it. I know it is somewhere on this escritoire, but as to where…

My mind is full of all sorts of imaginings, and my heart is so heavy of late that I find not a day goes by that I do not have the headache and must retire to my couch in the afternoon, and you know the cause!

Please, do not mention what I tell you to Roxton, or to Lucian. But why do I say this to you, when I know you know that I know that they both know! Ugh. It is my misfortune to have a brother who sees and knows everything, and a husband who is complacent enough to let him do so!

Lucian could not dissimulate if he tried. And he never would with Roxton. I do believe that is what makes them such good friends. Indeed, I believe my husband's first loyalty is to my brother, and then to me! No! Do not refute it. You are as bad as they, with your utter devotion to Roxton, and loyalty to my husband, though you both pretend to be annoyed by the other. Ha! That is a ruse. You secretly enjoy baiting each other, and my brother he enjoys watching you.

And you will laugh to the point of falling off your chair when I tell you what an imbecile I've been. I can hardly believe it myself, if you want the truth. And when I think back on my fears and actions now, I agree with my own assessment. But let me tell you, so you have the entire picture in your mind's eye, before your eyes they fill with tears of laughter at your sister's ridiculousness.

I began to suspect Lucian of having a little diversion across the river. Yes! Lucian unfaithful! There! I have inked it for you to read and your eyes to widen with the shock of disbelief that I could dare suspect my husband of straying.

After I recovered from my great shock and anger to think this might be true, I fell into a deep melancholy at the thought of him building a little nest with some light-skirt half my age, and twice as pretty. I could not rise from my couch for days. When Lucian did not come looking for me the first night I was not in our bed, my melancholy deepened, thinking my fears justified. For why would he not seek me out when we have shared a bed for as many years as you and my brother, unless his interest it was now directed elsewhere? The second night he did come looking, and stood in his nightshirt and cap peering down at me, holding the taper within an inch of my nose—I thought my hair it would catch alight! And what do I say and do when he asks what is the matter with me and to come to bed? I burst into tears and tell him to go away! And what does he do? He quietly goes away! Not a word to me! Impossible man!

So do you see why my fears that he must have a mistress intensified and my headache became unbearable? How could I tell him why I was so upset, when I feared the answer might be the one I did not want to hear at all? But I could not go on with the agony of not knowing one way or the other, so on the third day I resolved to discover if my fears were true or not.

You will be shocked by what I did, I know it, but dear sister, you cannot know what agony I was in! You would never do such a thing, for your confidence in your husband is so deeply rooted that I doubt you have ever entertained the notion of him ever straying, even with his eyes, and he such a great rake before he married you! And why should you have a single doubt? The fires still burn just as intensely for you and my brother—I see it when I am in your company. Such depth of feeling enthralls and nauseates me in equal measure.

But we are not talking of your marriage but mine, and my stupid fears manifesting themselves in ridiculous actions. Please, you must promise not to breathe a word of this to Roxton or to Lucian. My brother he will have a good chuckle at my expense, and my husband will think his wife is deranged. I will never hear the end of his grumbles of incredulity that I could ever question his fidelity.

This is what I did. I had Lucian followed. Yes, I set a spy on to him, day and night for a week. He could not step outside the house without this person two steps behind him. He became his shadow, and wherever he went, whatever he did, the spy he was there too.

Am I not the most wretched of wives to do this? But I tell you when the spy he reported all that he saw after just one week of being Lucian's shadow, my mind was far from put at ease. My suspicions they were inflamed further and I fell weeping upon my couch. The spy told me that not only had my husband strayed across to the left bank, but that he visited the same house upon three separate days, and spent two hours within its walls on each of these days.

The spy he had even managed to procure the name of the owner of this house. That a man owned it did not lessen my fears. For all I knew then, this man could have been a pimp and the woman Lucian was seeing his bawd. But the story it becomes worse, and my fears justified when the spy told me that Lucian he was not the only gentleman to visit the house, and often.

So now I am thinking that it is not a mistress he has, but that he is visiting a brothel! For some reason this made me feel a little better, to think his wandering was not restricted to one woman, but then of course I reversed this notion, for if he was seeing multiple women what did that say about him and about our marriage? And oh! a thousand other impossible things that go through the mind when it is in turmoil.

Please, you must try to read this without giggling, Antonia! For I am very sure, as night follows day, that is precisely what you are doing, to think of Lucian visiting a brothel. In truth, the man could be standing outside such an establishment and have no idea as to its function.

But I have not told you the rest of this sorry tale, and why I am such an imbecile to even have one bad thought about my dear husband. But you must remember—at the time his behavior was so odd that my fears he was up to something were justified, even if those fears headed down completely the wrong alleyway!

So to clip a long tale short. This house was not a brothel. It was not even occupied by a woman of ill repute. I had the spy discover all this for me by throwing more coins at him to find a way of gaining entry to this establishment. It took him a few days more, and in those few days my headache was so bad, my apprehension so acute, that I hardly ate or slept. And do you think Lucian he noticed my deteriorating state? It took our son remarking at dinner one night why I was not eating what was put before me for his father to repeat the same question to me, and then add that if I was not partial to the slice of pheasant pie on my plate, perhaps Evelyn he would like to have it; after all, there was no point in wasting good pie. To which I threw down my napkin and stormed out of the room to a big silence from my husband and our son.

But their enormous appetites are nothing new to you. It infuriates me beyond measure that those two could eat until they burst and they would still be as thin as a rapier, when I need only glance at an éclair and my arms they are a little tighter in my silk sleeves.

But returning to Lucian's visits to this house and my ridiculous fears. And now as I am writing this, I am starting to giggle, too. Not only with relief that my dear husband is as devoted as always, but thinking on what he was doing, and why. So now you have my permission to laugh with me. Though promise me again, you will not laugh at Lucian, or breathe a word.

So who were these men coming and going from this house, and why was my husband one of them? It turns out this house is a club, and its members pay a small annual fee, to come and go as they please, for use and upkeep of the refreshment rooms, and of course, the playing areas within the walled garden at the back of the house. The spy found all this out when he made an attempt to enter the premises and was told that the clientele was exclusive, though not limited to our kind, as most of the gentlemen are from the professions. I suspect Lucian thought that by finding a club on the other side of the river there was less likelihood of him being found out or meeting someone known to us. Well, he did not figure on having a jealous and suspicious wife wanting to know his every move!

So what is this club in a house on the left bank with a high-walled garden that requires upkeep and has an exclusive membership, where only men are permitted to enter, and, I dare say, the only female within fifty yards, is the maid cleaning the cups from the table?

It is a Boules club! Boules! Antonia! Boules. As Father Michael is my confessor, I tell you the truth when I say Lucian is spending two hours of his day three times a week in playing at boules with lawyers and physicians, and the like! *Mon Dieu!* Of all the things for him to be doing, and what I thought he was doing, he is doing nothing more than playing boules.

Oh, Antonia, when the spy he told me this, I burst into such tears of joy and incredulity that my women thought I was having some sort of fit. My stays were too tight and I could not breathe from laughing with relief. My headache was gone in an instant and I was up off my couch and demanding a bath and my best gown, so that I could look my best for when Lucian he returned later that day. I even sent down to the kitchen to prepare his favorite dish of garlic fowl.

I will not bore you with the details of my dear husband spending his time playing at boules in such a secretive manner. He has such a competitive nature where games are concerned, and I am sure it is only this nature that made him an expert swordsman. And again you must say nothing of this to Roxton, who will surely tease my dear husband, if not in so many words, but enough for Lucian to wonder how he came to know of his little secret.

So now you have wiped your eyes dry of tears of mirth, I lay the blame for my poor health and unfounded suspicions during this episode, and Lucian's obsession for boules, at your dainty feet, dearest sister. It is, after all, all your fault! For why does Lucian practice and practice his bowling? Because of some ridiculous wager between the two of you! No doubt said by you as a throw-away comment and instantly forgotten, but taken up by Lucian as a challenge and one he is determined to win. No matter it is for the sum of ten pounds—what is that to both of you? It is the winning that matters to Lucian. Of course, I told him that he is bound to beat you at this game, which made him very happy. But in truth I do not believe it, because you are the better player, and because Lucian, I think, does not see as well as he pretends, and thus everything past his outstretched arm is blurry. So he has convinced himself he can win, and no one else.

So now that you know I am a foolish woman to think my marriage it was ever in jeopardy of being unhappy, and that I am no longer haunted by unfounded fears, I must tell you that my headache has returned, and perhaps even worse than before, and that what, rather who, brought it back with alarming rapidity is my son!

As a mother of sons, my dearest sister, only you can share the worry I have about my darling boy. From the moment of his birth until this morning, every day of his life has been my constant joy and my daily concern. Fathers have concern, too, but they do not worry as we do, and sometimes I wonder if they even think about their children from one week to the next!

Today I am worried that Evelyn he does not show the slightest inclination for the usual masculine pursuits that any boy his age should. He hates physical exertion of any sort, though he is not such a bad swordsman. So his father says. And Lucian should know, he being the premier swordsman in his day. He says that what Evelyn does not exert himself in movement, he does so in placement of his rapier. And it is in this way he is able to best his opponent. Apparently, this placement it is not such an easy thing to do, and that Roxton he was good at such skill. Lucian tells me not to worry, that Evelyn will hold his own if it comes to a duel, or if he is set upon by a pack of ruffians, he may find himself beaten up, but they won't best him with a sword.

That is supposed to give me peace of mind?

And he does not join the hunt, or shoot, or place a wager on any of the animal baiting as all young men his age do. He prefers to haunt chamber orchestras, operas and musical gatherings, taking with him his violin. He often will go to the Tuileries when there are the stalls, and so the greatest number of people parading about, people that we know. He sets up his little lectern with his sheets of music, and plays for the common man, as if he is a beggar and not the nephew of a duke. Why? What is the purpose of drawing attention to himself in this way, Antonia? Why does he shame himself in such a fashion? Does he care nothing for his family name? His ancient relatives? That his mamma, daughter of a marquis, granddaughter of a duke, and sister of a duke—and not just any duke, but Roxton—is mortified that her son is performing in public in this way? Does he care nothing for my feelings, my shame?

I demanded Lucian order his son to stop putting on these shameful public displays, to counsel him about what he owes his name, and how these public performances make his dear mamma take to her bed. And what does Lucian do? He does not do as I ask. He does not tell Evelyn that he is shaming himself and his family, and more importantly endangering his mamma's health! I can hardly bring myself to ink it here what he did do, but I will, for you. Instead, Lucian he asks Evelyn how much money the public threw into his cap, and if there is enough coinage to buy a good bottle of wine. And then they laugh about it together like two naughty children. Which infuriates me more than anything! And not one word of caution to his son passes Lucian's lips. It is mortifying in the extreme.

And do not get me started on Evelyn and females, because there is nothing to say!

I ask myself why he does not debauch and chase women and be as a man? Which is the normal behavior for our sons at such an age, is it not? Why, while you are in England, he Alston is getting for himself a reputation in the salons for his penchant for a particular Opera dancer —or is she a singer? No matter. What matters is, he is getting a reputation! Which is as it should be for the son of a duke. But the only reputation my son is gaining is as a suspected *petit maître*! I tell you, Antonia, I am mortified, and secretly devastated if it be true because I will never have grandchildren. And I must have grandchildren, for what is left to us in old age if we do not have little ones to worry ourselves over?

Can life be so cruel to me? Can Evelyn be so cruel to his mamma as to prefer his own kind to that of sharing his couch with a woman? Of course Lucian says my head it is full of unfounded fears and nonsense, and that I should stop listening to the gossip at Julie Charmond's salons. He says he has it on the best authority that our son is a regular visitor to a particular brothel not far from here that caters exclusively to noblemen. I told him I did not believe that for a moment and for me to believe it I must have proof. Lucian of course has no proof, and he stormed out of my morning toilette, grumbling about his word not being good enough and his face all flushed.

Now, thinking back on that conversation, I believe that this best authority is himself! And that his reaction of storming out of my boudoir was perhaps because Lucian, too, engaged a spy, and to watch our son. And this because he, like me, was worried that his son might not care for women in that way. But discovering our son visits a brothel catering to noblemen who desire women has made Lucian less concerned about Evelyn's predilections, but too embarrassed to tell me how he discovered this information, and what I would think of him setting a person to spy on our son.

Mon Dieu, but my family are all imbeciles in our own ways, and again I am giggling thinking about our silliness.

Antonia, I cannot continue to write another stroke. My head it is splitting, this time from laughter, which also makes me weak. But it should please you I am, we all are, very happy. But missing you and the family.

All my love and kisses to Henri-Antoine, to Roxton, and to you, my dearest sister. Please hurry home.

Yours devotedly,
Estée

The Most Honorable Marquess of Alston, Bess House, Lake Windermere, Cumbria, England, to His Grace The Most Noble Duke of Roxton, Hotel Roxton, Rue St. Honoré, Paris, France.

Bess House, Lake Windermere, Cumbria, England
November, 1769

Dearest Papa, I trust this short missive finds you and Mamma in your customary good health, and Harry in better health than your last letter, in which you reported he had suffered two seizures in two weeks.

That was before Jack Cavendish went to stay with you, and I trust that with his best friend for company, he is not worn thin. Jack is a lively boy but also good-natured, as you have no doubt already discovered. I have every faith in him lifting Harry's spirits, and perhaps diverting him enough from his illness to enjoy just being a boy, and less the introspective invalid. Please give him a kiss and my love. Tell him his big brother has been practicing his archery skills, so that when I come to Paris, he will get his chance to increase his lead against me. I believe he has three bull's-eyes to my one.

I don't know when was the last time you had the opportunity to visit Bess House here in Cumbria. As I have no recollection of ever setting foot this far north, and Mamma has never mentioned this place, I can only assume you have never been to the Elizabethan ancestral pile of your father's mother, the 4th Duchess of Roxton, the Lady Elizabeth Strang Leven as she was at the time she resided here. There is a portrait of her upon the wall, and another of her brother and his two closest male cousins, all fine-looking fellows but for their silly hair. All are wearing those long wigs preferred in the time of the Merry Monarch, with enough hair upon their scalps to cover the bald pates of six maidens! Such poodles. But your grandmother is a fine-looking woman, with dark eyes that hold your attention and thus make her unforgettable. If I am not much mistaken, you inherited your eyes from her.

But I am sure you are not interested in your grandmother's eyes, or what I can tell you about the estate that you do not already read in the monthly reports sent to you by the estate's manager. What I will remark upon, as an interested third party, is that the Dunnes keep the place in good order, though despite their slavish devotion, the topiary gardens could do with the advice of a reputable gardener, and the muscle power of a team of his men to clip the leafy structures back to their former glory. Thus, I have given permission for the Dunnes to employ such men, and also to rebuild the jetty that was burned down around the time of the rebellion of '45, when the house was occupied by rebels and then housed the army for a time.

I request your permission to bring my family here to live. Yes, father, my family. For I am determined to make a success of my marriage. You will be pleased to read it is no longer a marriage in name only. To be sure it was an arranged union that came about in the most trying of circumstances, but since bringing Deborah here, how our marriage came about is now irrelevant to me. I hope, once she is made aware of this circumstance, my wife, too, will think it a trifle of a thing. What matters is the here and now, and the future.

I know at the time we were wed, the criteria as to Deborah's suitability to be my bride were her lineage and her age, with no regard for her appearance, her disposition, or her intelligence. Our thoughts and feelings were disregarded as unimportant.

And yet, may I venture to state the obvious. When you married mamma, it must have been all about feelings. You married a woman who could live up to your exulted rank, and to your expectations, a woman possessed not only of great physical beauty, but whose thoughts and deeds reflected her inner beauty, and whose superior mind was in accord with yours.

I do not dwell on these matters to cause you pain but to reassure you and Mamma that despite the circumstances of our marriage, I am quite certain I, too, have found in Deborah a mate that lives up to my expectations in every way. I hope this will ease your minds. Now if only I can live up to my wife's expectations, as a husband and as a father to our future children, I will be content. Is that how you feel with Mamma—content? It is a word I never thought to use in relation to my marriage, and yet now it is the only word I hope to use for my future with Deborah.

Which brings me to the reason for this letter. My apologies, but I cannot tell you when we will be able to travel to Paris. I would like to be able to say we are on our way. But we are not. I am not about to cut short time spent with my bride to satisfy the whims of a French lawyer, and the lies of a Farmer-General's petulant daughter. I will come when I am ready—when we are ready.

I cannot leave here until I am confident Deborah will accept my little deception, for she still does not know who I am, and I have yet to find the right moment to confide in her—to confess to her. I hesitate to do this just yet. She needs more time to know me thoroughly and thus when I finally reveal my true nobility, will be able to judge for herself that I could never be the libidinous monster portrayed in the French newssheets by those seeking to destroy my credibility and the good name of my family.

Thus I politely decline your request that I present myself in Paris at my earliest convenience. Instead, I crave your indulgence to see that my wife and I are at a delicate stage in this the early weeks of our union. When I am confident my wife's trust in me is complete, and I have summoned the courage to tell her the truth, only then will I leave here and return to Paris to face my accusers.

I am sorry to cause you and Mamma unwarranted anxiety, but I am confident you both understand how important this is to me, and to the future of the Roxton dukedom.

Your loving son,
Julian

Sir Gerald Cavendish Bt., Abbey Wood via Bisley, Gloucester-shire, England, to His Grace The Most Noble Duke of Roxton, Hotel Roxton, Rue St. Honoré, Paris, France.

Abbey Wood via Bisley, Gloucestershire, England
February, 1770

My Lord Duke,

It is with grave concern that I report the most unfortunate news. I trust that upon reading this letter you will not think badly of your correspondent, for I am merely the messenger, and as such, am as disappointed, nay, furious, with my sister—if I can indeed still call her that after her appalling lack of manners and finer feelings—as must you be upon reading this missive.

I am most saddened to tell you, my lord Duke, that no amount of persuasion on my part will see my sister leave her house in Bath and journey to Paris to take her rightful place at the side of her esteemed husband. I spent many hours endeavoring to press upon her the duty she owes to your family, but in vain. She stubbornly will not see any argument but her own. Upon my third visit in as many days she barred me entrance to her house. Me! Her brother, denied access by her servants. I am very sure you must be as horrified as was I at such a circumstance, and to think these menials had the audacity to turn the key in the lock against me, and leave me standing in the street awaiting a reply. The impudence of such an action almost made me turn heel and walk away. But then I remembered the greater need, that of your son, Lord Alston, to have his wife join him in Paris, to show family unity at this most unsettling of times. Thus I waited upon the pavement a good five minutes, being stared at by a number of persons going about their business, for my sister to allow me entry. Imagine my disgust when told, by shouts coming through the door, no less, that permission was refused and there was nothing to add to my conversation of the previous two visits.

I then called upon Deborah's physician, in the hopes Dr. Medlow would prove more reasonable, and answer the mystery as to the illness being suffered by my sister. The man would tell me nothing other than my sister was indeed ill. He had the impudence to add that it would be best for her health and well-being if I stayed away from Milsom Street! I can well imagine your look of disgust, dear Duke, to read that a member of the medical fraternity had the audacity to offer advice to a baronet! I threatened to have Medlow struck off the register. I made him aware of just who he was defying—in truth you, Your Grace. But nothing would move him to utter one syllable more than what he had already told me. And he bid me good day!

When I had visited Deborah upon those two occasions and was permitted into her presence, she remained prostrate on her couch, and did not give me the courtesy of a welcome, and barely opened one eye to take in my person. It was as if even this small flicker of recognition were too much for her to bear, for she promptly pushed a handkerchief to her mouth and turned her face into the cushion, with all the drama to the action worthy of Mrs. Woffington!

I am of the opinion that it is all a ruse to bide her time while she consults an attorney sympathetic to her cause in seeking a separation from her husband. For that is what she intends, Your Grace. I am still in a state of shock at the thought! It is beyond my comprehension to understand why she would want to distance herself from such an illustrious family. No amount of persuasion on my part, in particular in reinforcing the happy news that one day she will be a duchess, and not just any duchess but the Duchess of Roxton, received from her nothing more than a groan, as if the very notion gave her physical pain. I then told her in no uncertain terms that even to initiate such proceedings will lead to her ruin, and in so doing, she will ruin the good name of Cavendish, and give the Roxton Dukedom unwarranted attention. To which she merely proceeded to turn her face away altogether and muffled unintelligibly into her cushion, which her lady's maid interpreted as a wish for me to leave her mistress alone with her suffering.

I beg Your Grace to believe me that while she is my sister, my loyalty is and always will be to you and your family. I dare to seek your forgiveness for my sister's outrageous behavior. I trust her unconscionable behavior will in no way reflect upon my person and my loyalty, and that the invitation your dear duchess extended to my wife and me, to join you in Paris for the marriage celebration of the French Dauphin to the Austrian Princess Marie Antoinette, remains a welcome one.

Lady Mary and I look forward to joining you and the dear Duchess in the spring.

Your most obedient and humble servant,
Gerald Cavendish Bt.

Mme la Duchesse d'Roxton, Hotel Roxton, Rue St. Honoré, Paris, France, to Mr. Martin Ellicott, Esq., Moran House, the Bath Road, Avon, England.

Hotel Roxton, Rue St. Honoré, Paris
March, 1770

Dearest Martin,

I am counting the days until you join us. I am being selfish and wish you were here now, before the rest of the family come, so we could have you all to ourselves for a few days at least. But I hope that will still happen, when the others they all go away at the end of the Parisian celebrations for the marriage of *Le Roi's* grandson to his Austrian princess.

No one but Monseigneur knows me better than you, my dearest friend. And so when I tell you that only a sennight ago our cherished hope-filled wish once again came to naught, you understand how this has left me inconsolable. I was convinced that this little one would hold on to life and grow, and we would be blessed with an infant at the beginning of the autumn. But sadly it was not to be and I lost this *bébé* at eleven weeks.

This time we told no one I was *enceinte*. Only my women knew, as they would, and we prayed for what must now surely be the impossible. We had planned to tell Julian, had the *bébé* grown past the first months. I did not confide in Estée or in Vallentine, only you. For do you remember me telling you about their reaction to the news when I was pregnant less than two years ago? I was stunned to hear them both say M'sieur le Duc was too old to be a new Papa, Estée even daring to suggest that at our age we should not be fornicating at all! She used the word indecent. *Incroyable*! I do not care to know what goes on in the privacy of their bedchamber, and therefore what goes on in mine is none of their business either. Although, you will think me naughty, but not unlike me, when I tell you I replied to Estée that for us every night it is as if the honeymoon it has never ended. My poor sister she almost fainted and fell off the chaise at that! And I admit I laughed, and so did Renard when I told him of my taunt later that evening.

My sons they are the world to me and perhaps a little more so now with this latest miscarriage. They are far apart in age—the eldest so wanted and celebrated, the youngest wanted just as much and such a long time in coming, that they console me after the heartbreak of five little ones (and now a sixth) taken from us before they were barely formed, and for reasons only God knows. Not as my grandmother would have it, and so it seems also Estée is of the same opinion, because of the age disparity between Renard and me. An absurd and spiteful theory. Is it wrong of me to wish she had lived long enough to see the birth of Henri-Antoine? Just so I could spite her? No! That is an awful thing to wish and you must forgive me. I am still grieving and not altogether myself. I promise I will be mended by the time you arrive, because you always make me feel better.

A letter from me would not be the same, would it not, without talk of my little boy and his seizures. He worries us constantly. Not only because of his monthly, sometimes weekly, seizures, which send his thin little body rigid, his dark eyes wide, and me into heart palpitations, because I wonder if this will be the one in which his breathing it stops altogether! But Dr. Bailey remains confident that with age and skillful management, the seizures will lessen in frequency and severity. We can only take his word for it.

M'sieur le Duc, as you know, is not one for public displays of emotion, and so he hides well how greatly Henri-Antoine's affliction affects him. As ever he is calm and in control, which has taken a lifetime's practice, though I know inside he is falling apart. I truly believe that it is Renard's voice which has a calming effect on our son. I am not imagining it when I say that while there is the same severity, the episode it does not last as long when he speaks so soothingly to Henri-Antoine. Dr. Bailey is of this same opinion.

So while I wring my hands and pace out of sight of my dearest little one, there is M'sieur le Duc sitting by his side, holding his son's fingers, and stroking his smooth brow with a cool hand. And all the while he is talking to him in a gentle tone, and in English, which for some unknown reason deepens his already deep voice. To hear him speak in such a soothing manner swells my heart and brings tears to my eyes. Henri-Antoine has never said to either of us that he hears what his Papa says to him, only that he knows his Papa is there with him. I do not know the half of what Renard says to him, not because I do not understand his English, but because I am so overwrought I can barely think at all. But do you know, Martin,

M'sieur le Duc's voice has the same effect on me, and soon I, too, am calmer.

We, Henri-Antoine and I, listen to the stories of Renard's boyhood, when he and Vallentine were very naughty at Eton, or the time on the Grand Tour when they raced camels along the banks of the Nile; or when they took the Mont Cenis pass, carried by the Marrons, who are the local villagers, in special chairs, and were so intent on racing each other in the snow, that the Marrons lost their footing from running and they all almost went over the side of the mountain pass and tumbled to their deaths. And all this he tells Henri-Antoine in a voice as if it is an everyday occurrence. And what breaks my heart is that he ends these tales with the same wish every time—that when Henri-Antoine he is older he will do the same naughty things with his best friend, and nothing will make his Papa happier than to read his letters of their naughtiness.

But now I have another worry, and, Martin, you must be truthful when you see M'sieur le Duc, and tell me if you think him altered and perhaps not as well-looking since you saw him at Christmastime. He will not tell me what is the matter, and says it is nothing. That he having turned two-and-sixty it is natural to have more regular visits from his physicians. But I know he is hiding something from me! I know it! You tell me—when was the last time he did not go for an early morning ride, if not before breakfast, then mid-morning at least? And these past three months he has only been in the saddle a dozen times or less. And his breathing is not as it should be. Though he does his best to hide it from me! Me! Why? Why should he suddenly start hiding things from me when he has never done so before? So you will be truthful when you see him and tell me that I am not imagining that he is a little out of breath and looking tired

Of course, it could all be because of the great strain on him of this ridiculous court case and accusations against Julian, that it presses upon his mind. I too am out of breath, but from anger to think a Farmer-General has the impudence to take my son to court, and for a thing I know he did not commit. To think it is all over the newssheets here and they allow such slander to be printed is even beyond what the English newssheets would permit. I am convinced there is some deeper purpose to this than just a silly little girl's infatuation for my son, and a Farmer-General's wish to elevate his family into the ranks of the nobility—two things that are as likely to happen as cows flying past my window!

You tell me our son is incapable of such actions as are described in the French press, that he is too honorable, and has too much pride, that it would never enter his head to want to seduce any girl, least of all one of the bourgeoisie. And you know our son as well as his parents! I think you also know too that Julian he is a prude and morally chaste. Had not M'sieur le Duc confided in me about our son's affair with that Russian diplomat's pretty wife, me I would think him completely ignorant of the bedroom when he went on his honeymoon! But I am glad he was not, for his wife's sake. Which leads me to tell you that I treasure the letter you sent us upon Julian's return from Cumbria with Deborah.

It made us very happy to know that finally they are truly husband and wife. That he whisked her off to the wilds of Lake Windermere for a proper honeymoon bodes well for the start of their marriage, yes? That you tell me our daughter-in-law is in love with Julian makes me feel much better about the union. As you know I was very unhappy that Renard married off Julian in such a way, and had Deborah not turned out to be to his liking, or he to hers, then I would have gladly seen them separated before the union it had been consummated.

That matters have not taken the turn we had hoped, with Deborah remaining in England, for what I believe is stubbornness, I cannot blame her. She has every right to her anger at Julian for deceiving her about his nobility. Why did he not find a moment while on the honeymoon to confess all to her? There is no better place than the marital bed for such a confession, and so I am mystified why my son he was not capable of such lover's talk with his bride? But he is young, and I suspect quite bashful, so he has still much to learn about being a lover and a husband that only self-confidence and time will rectify. I will not be an interfering mother, and pray they can sort the matter out between them, and before M'sieur le Duc he becomes truly angry with the behavior of both. I am all sympathy for his frustration with Julian's high-mindedness, but it is best he is his own man, and so I have told Renard.

Please do hurry to us. Henri-Antoine asks after his Uncle Martin. Julian could do with your wise counsel, for it is another voice to make him see reason. And Renard and I must have your support for the ordeal that is to come with the court case. And of course, Vallentine would not feel loved if I did not tease him and you support me to his detriment!

Bon voyage, mon cher et bon ami,
Antonia Roxton

The Most Honorable Marquess of Alston, Hotel Roxton, Rue St. Honoré, Paris, France, to Mr. Martin Ellicott, Esq., Moran House, the Bath Road, Avon, England.

Hotel Roxton, Rue St. Honoré, Paris
October, 1770

Dearest Martin, I have a son! A healthy baby boy who is perfect in every way, with a mop of dark hair and a pair of fine working lungs! His lusty cries are a joy to the ear, even at four in the morning, when he wakes his mamma and papa demanding to be fed. I do not mind in the least, and as Deb has insisted on suckling our son, he spends most of his time in bed with us, much to the consternation of Tante Estée, who cannot understand why we have not employed a wet nurse, and why, in the name of all that is sacred, we would want a screaming and demanding (her words, not mine) infant near us all the time.

But I cannot stop looking at him. I am still dazed with happiness to think he is mine, and I am a father. You can well imagine how dearest Papa feels to know there are now two generations to follow him.

But let me tell you that Deb is very well indeed. She endured a long labor, which I am told is normal with first pregnancies. And though she cursed me roundly, and I deserved it all, she was the bravest girl imaginable and is recovering very well indeed. The physician said it was a comparatively easy labor, all things considered, which bodes well for future pregnancies. Oh, it is not me you should scold for thinking of the children yet to come. It was Deb who was very pleased with herself, telling me what the physician had said to her!

Would it shock you to know I was with Deb throughout her ordeal? It was the most wondrous experience. I was fraught with such anxiety when her pains came on, and was suffering the agony of hearing her cries from the other side of the door, not knowing what was happening to her, and if she were in any danger. I think I paced the Turkey rug to threads!

It is all very well in hindsight to know Deb's cries were normal and not a sign she was in any danger, but at the time I was feeling utterly useless with all sorts of horrific imaginings going through my head that I thought I would faint. And then Papa said the most startling thing to me. He asked why I wasn't in there supporting my wife at such a time, and did I not want to witness the birth of my son? He would not have missed the experience of being at my birth for the world. My head nearly snapped off its neck at that, I can tell you. I must have glared at him like he had two heads, and it took Mamma laughing at me and telling me to stop being a block of wood, and to get in there with Deborah before it was too late. That was all the push I needed!

We have broken with tradition and given our son three names unrelated to the Roxton side of the family. Frederick, for Mamma's papa; George, for Deb's father; and Martin, for you, *mon parrain*. I hope you are as pleased with our son's names as we are, and indeed, as Papa and Mamma are, too.

To see Frederick cradled in his grandfather's arms brings tears to my eyes, for Papa's face takes on a healthy glow, there is that twinkle in his eye, and he looks his old self. Of course Mamma is completely smitten, and she is such a natural mother that she is already Frederick's firm favorite. Naturally, Henri-Antoine and Jack are ambivalent, and to see the boys screw up their noses and look at each other in mutual horror when Frederick begins to fuss, as if a baby's cries were akin to the plague, has all of us laughing heartily. How I wish you were here with us, and look forward to you joining us at Treat for Christmastime, and the christening.

Everyone sends their love. Deb in particular asked to be remembered to you.

A bientôt, mon cher parrain,
Julian

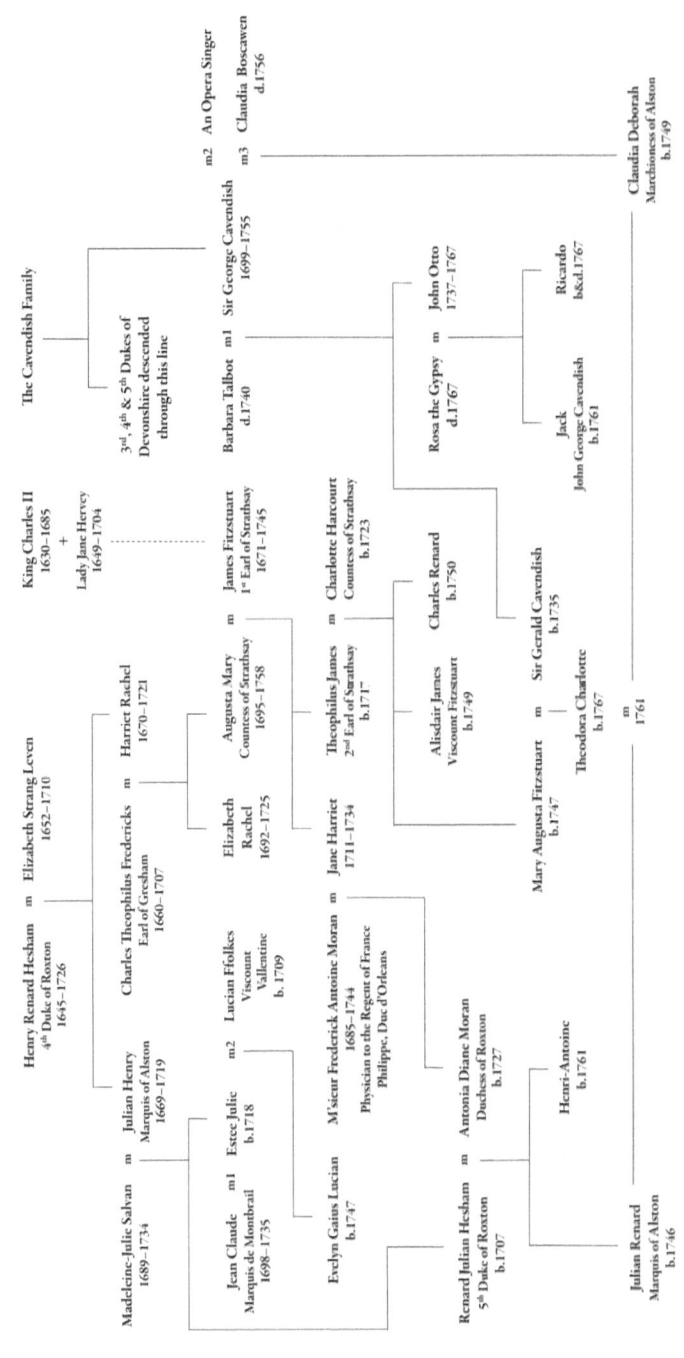

The Cavendish Family

King Charles II
1630–1685
+
Lady Jane Hervey
1649–1704

Henry Renard Hesham   m   Elizabeth Strang Leven
4th Duke of Roxton   1652–1710
1645–1726

3rd, 4th & 5th Dukes of
Devonshire descended
through this line

m2   An Opera Singer
m3   Claudia Boscawen
      d.1756

Julian Henry
Marquis of Alston
1669–1719

Charles Theophilus Fredericks   m   Harriet Rachel
Earl of Gresham   1670–1721
1660–1707

Barbara Talbot   m1   Sir George Cavendish
d.1740   1699–1755

James Fitzstuart
1st Earl of Strathsay
1671–1745

Madeleine-Julie Salvan   m
1689–1734

Lucian Ffolkes
Viscount
Vallentine
b.1709

Elizabeth
Rachel
1692–1725

Augusta Mary
Countess of Strathsay
1695–1758

Charlotte Harcourt
Countess of Strathsay
b.1723

John Otto
1737–1767

Rosa the Gypsy   m
d.1767

Jean Claude   m1   Estée Julie
Marquis de Montbrail   b.1718
1698–1735

Mi sieur Frederick Antoine Moran   m
1685–1744
Physician to the Regent of France
Philippe, Duc d'Orleans

Jane Harriet
1711–1734

Theophilus James
2nd Earl of Strathsay
b.171~

Charles Renard
b.1750

Alisdair James
Viscount Fitzstuart
b.1749

Jack
John George Cavendish
b.1761

Ricardo
b&d.1767

Evelyn Gains Lucian
b.1747

Antonia Diane Moran
Duchess of Roxton
b.1727

Mary Augusta Fitzstuart
b.1747

Sir Gerald Cavendish
b.1735

m
1761

Theodora Charlotte
b.1767

Renard Julian Hesham   m
5th Duke of Roxton
b.1707

Henri-Antoine
b.1761

Claudia Deborah
Marchioness of Alston
b.1749

Julian Renard
Marquis of Alston
b.1746

AUTUMN DUCHESS
LETTERS

Autumn Duchess Letter 1

His Grace The Most Noble Duke of Roxton, Treat via Alston, Hampshire, to The Most Honorable Marquess of Alston, Bess House, Lake Windermere, Cumbria.

Treat
November, 1773

My son, I am so proud of you, as a son, as a husband and father, and as a gentleman. You are the man I should have been at your age, but I did not fully embrace my destiny until I met your mother.

You will be a most worthy Duke of Roxton, and a much better nobleman than ever I was. That is as it should be. The next generation should always strive to be better than the last.

I applaud your strength of character to be your own man. You have had the burden of living in my shadow for so many years, and yet you have forged ahead with dignity and purpose to put your own stamp on your life, as you will do with the dukedom. I have every confidence in you upholding a legacy that stretches back to Good Queen

Bess. Long after you are gone, your descendants will remember you as a good and moral man, and an exemplary duke. I could ask for no finer man to succeed me.

You must not grieve excessively at my passing. You have a duty to look always to the future. That is our lot in life. For those of us born the eldest and who hold in trust great names and great estates for future generations, we cannot afford the luxury of being maudlin. We can look back with fondness and to ensure we do not repeat the mistakes of our forebears, but we must never look back with regret. It is our responsibility and obligation to look forward, to secure a brighter future for our sons.

In Deborah you have been blessed with a good, loving and devoted wife. She has given you three fine sons in as many years, and will give you more, of that I am convinced. For these reasons alone, she is deserving of your devotion. But you know as well as I that for a marriage to succeed it must be a true partnership. Your wife's personal happiness is paramount, as is investing in the time you share together, and as a family. Only in this way will your marriage remain strong, and serve you both and your children well in times of distress and sadness.

I came late to love and to marriage. I do not regret my earlier life, but every day since I wed your mother I have only looked forward, not back, and lived each day a little in awe of my good fortune.

I have no qualms in departing this earth when God deems me ready to enter the kingdom of Heaven. I know in my heart that I will see you again in the next life, where I will be waiting for you, and for my family to join me, but most of all, waiting for your mother to be with me for eternity.

You knew I could not write you a final letter without mentioning her.

Your mother is the sun and we merely the planets that revolve around her. She is the giver of light and warmth and unconditional love. Without her we would be living in a cold, dark place.

The irony is that with my passing you will, for a time, live in this cold, dark place. Your mother will suffer the loss of me most keenly, so keenly that I worry for her sanity. Just thinking about such a consequence has kept me from breathing my last, to the astonishment and confounding of my physicians, who look to the physical signs of my deterioration without taking into account that my mind is resilient and tenacious. It will simply not listen to learned medical opinion and shall continue to have command over my body until my heart or my lungs or both can no longer do as they are ordered, and I do, indeed, stop breathing.

While your mother is possessed of a fine intelligence and is able to converse, argue and declaim on all manner of intellectual subjects usually deemed beyond the capability of her fair sex, she is utterly weak-minded when it comes to matters of the heart. I am supremely grateful for her emotional weakness. Feelings to her are everything, and I, who was raised to sublimate sentiment for the greater good of my venerable position as peer of this realm, am thankful every day that she loves unconditionally and feels so fiercely and so deeply.

But that is no consolation to you, who upon my passing will be left to deal with an inconsolable grieving widow. And because your mother feels every emotion with such intensity, she will be excessively fragile in mind. This, of course, will affect you and your family in every way imaginable.

I wish it were not so for your sake. But for mine, I cannot but be ever thankful that she came into my life when she did. We have been together more years than she has lived without me. Since her eighteenth birthday she has known no other life, no other companion, than me. I have self-ishly kept her with me, always. Neither of us would have had it any other way. But for her, who was so young when we wed, it has meant that despite having an independent will and a keen mind, she has never been required to be emotionally self-sufficient. Though, up until my illness, I would not have considered this at all necessary to our lives, because I cannot conceive of life without her.

To my great relief and her everlasting sadness my terminal illness means I will never have to live without her.

But she must live without me. Do you understand, Julian? She must LIVE. She must go on living, and for many, many years. You are not the man who can make her see that, so do not try to do so. I pray there is one such out there who is worthy, worthy of her, and who can make her see that life is worth living after all.

You must not allow the responsibility of your mother and her grief to be a millstone about your neck. You are to live, too—for your wife and your children, those born and those yet to come. I know you and Deborah and your family will have long, happy and fulfilling lives, and that fills me with joy. You have allowed me a peaceable passing, one of contentment, and without a worry for the future. That is a fine gift for a proud parent.

Do not despair, my dearest boy. I go to a better place, where I will be welcomed and reunited with my dearest parents. And when God wills it, your mother will join me. I hold to that, and it is a great comfort.

I love you.
Your dearest Papa

[Roxton to Antonia—his last letter. Believed to have been written some months before his death in 1774.]

My love, for too long have I put off the writing of this letter. For too long have I fooled myself that perhaps I would never need to. For too long have I permitted myself to accept as true, as you have never waived in your belief, that I am M'sieur le Duc d'Roxton. As if my ancient nobility was somehow armor that made me, at least in your eyes, indestructible. Ah, my love, self-delusion is ever bittersweet.

But I shall be ever grateful to whatever alignment of the stars brought you—my radiant elfin beauty—into my life. Since the day we wed you must know that I have been your devoted servant. Never did I give another thought to the years that separated us in age. You are my wife, my constant companion, my only love, and I am, and have always been, utterly in love with you.

Each day with you has been lived as a year, each hour as a day. I wanted our life together to last for a thousand life-times, to spend as many hours in your joyous company as was possible. You who have not only been the love of my life, but a most wonderful mother to our sons—two fine gentlemen who are a daily source of pride and wonder. I never thought I would be a father, and to such sons, but they are yours, and I see you in them every day. In their mannerisms, in their beauty, and in their hearts and minds. But for all the time I have spent in their company, and in the company of our family and friends, it is the time alone with you that I cherish most. Those precious hours when there were just the two of us, in the library or in our bed half-asleep, me waking with the dawn, you sleeping contentedly in my arms, persuaded me that perhaps our time together could stretch on without end.

Our yearly visits to Swan Island had me almost convinced of this. If there is a paradise on earth, we found it on that island, did we not, *mignonne*? We had such carefree, happy times there. It allowed us to create the blissful illusion we had all the time in the world, and the world was ours.

I always thought that with you by my side anything was possible, and for the longest time everything was.

That I am soon to join my parents has brought the difference in our ages into sharp relief, and the pain of being separated from you is acute. I feel it beyond words. It is much more terrible than any physical discomfort I have suffered. That is as nothing. The sense of loss of being without you was so devastating that for one selfish moment I wished we were closer in age so that I might know the wait for you to join me would be a short one.

But the moment passed, and I realize that with you I have experienced such joy, such unconditional love and devotion that my life is blessed beyond what most men experience in a lifetime, or ten men in ten lifetimes. And so I go willingly and contented beyond this mortal existence to meet my maker, there to await you to join me. For me it will be but a blink of an eye, but for you…

Writing this letter is the most difficult task I have ever undertaken. Not because I have any difficulty in expressing my feelings for you, or what you mean to me, or how you have enriched my life in so many ways, but because I know what you must endure after I leave you.

This will not help ease your suffering, but I tell you this because I must. Perhaps, as the days pass into years, you will find some comfort in these words.

The irony is that with the coming of death, one spends one's remaining time reflecting on life! And life for me truly began the day I carried you into my house on the Rue St. Honoré with a bullet in your shoulder. Until the moment you were shot by that rogue, I had lived life, and well, but I had never realized that the life I was leading was emotionally mundane. I had ever engaged my feelings in only the most superficial of ways. You, my darling dear, opened my eyes to this startling state of affairs in a single moment, when I thought I might forever have lost you, and with it the opportunity to acquaint myself better with you. Even then, at that moment when I placed you on the sofa and we waited for the physician, there was a flicker of something more, something unsettling that I was not prepared to acknowledge for the longest time, but which you, despite your tender years, knew beyond doubt was love at first sight. I can laugh about it now, and shake my head at your indefatigability to believe we were meant to be together, and my stubborn refusal to know that my heart beat faster in your presence because I was in love with you.

I am still in love with you, and my heart still does beat faster when you enter a room, see me and smile as if it is the first time we have seen each other in a very long time, when in fact it was only an hour earlier that we parted at the dinner table. And when you rush straight up to me in a cloud of silks and soft perfume to press yourself against me, chin tilted up to receive a kiss you know I cannot refuse you, regardless of who is in the room, my heart not only beats faster, it sings with the joy of knowing you love me so very much.

You who have always understood me, accepted me as I am, and loved me unconditionally, and so fiercely that now, even as I write this, my hand shakes with over-whelming emotion. How is it that you alone were able to see beyond my arrogance to the man who wanted—no, needed—the love and loyalty of an honest woman, who could provide him a safe haven, a home. You know I do not speak of bricks and mortar, but of the heart—your heart, my darling, where I have lived a most happy and contented man, nourished by the love you have for me, for over a quarter of a century.

And now the time is almost upon us for me to leave you —there I have said it in ink—and still I am in denial. My body, such as it is, tells me to let go, to give myself up to the inevitable so that I can be at peace. I know I will then cross to a better place, that I will see my father who was lost to me when I was only twelve years old, and my mother, a most devoted and loving parent whom I also lost too early, and mourned deeply.

Yet, my mind wants me to hold on, and tries to convince me that even one more day with you by my side is worth the eternity that awaits me with my loved ones. I will hold on with all the strength I can muster—for you. So that you will have one fewer day to grieve. So that you will not suffer the desolation and unimaginable grief of us being parted on this earth.

You do not say it. We do not discuss it. It is as if by main-

taining our silence it will go away of its own accord. But I
see it reflected in your lovely eyes—oh, how I worship
those sparkling emerald-green jewels—when you think
me distracted or resting. I have always enjoyed watching
you in conversation, how you have this wonderful effect
on others. A light comes into their eyes, they smile, and
they feel better for just having spent time in your
company. And that, too, fills my heart with joy. You have
always had a gift for making others happy and at ease, and
when they take their leave of you I see they have a greater
sense of self-worth.

How can I tell you not to grieve? I know you will. A love
such as ours does not end here nor should it be denied.
Were I in your position I would have been inconsolable,
demented with grief, and unable to live with any sense of
the ordinary, long ago. And yet you have done your
utmost to ensure our life carries on as usual, for me, and
for our sons and our family, and you have done this for
three interminably long years. For that alone I prostrate
myself at your feet, humbled by your strength of character
and forbearance.

What I ask of you, my most precious darling, is that when
I close my eyes for the final time you use that strength of
character to continue to live. How am I to wait for you
knowing you live in misery and despair all because my
infirmity and age took me from you before you were ready
for me to leave you? You know I will be waiting for you to
join me, that once you do we will have eternity together.
So these few short years apart will be as nothing. So do
not waste them in grieving for me. You must live for our
sons and our grandchildren, all of whom need you.

And when you can shed no more tears, I want you to
open your thoughts to the possibility of loving and being
loved by another. And though this foolish old satyr is
gripped by an unreasonable jealousy at the mere thought

of his beauty in the arms of another, I urge you to take a lover. You, my heart's delight, are a sensual creature deserving of every attention an attentive lover can provide. I even dare to hope you may find another to love. Someone who will cherish you and laugh with you. Someone with whom you can snuggle up under the covers and lie content.

For your own sake, my dearest darling, please live and love as we lived and loved, surrounded by our family and friends, and you the center of it all.

I will not say *adieu* but *au revoir*. I shall have your favorite chaise ready, the pieces in place on the backgammon board between us, and there I will sit, resplendent in black velvet and silk, twirling my quizzing glass, waiting patiently for you to join me—forever.

Renard

[Antonia Roxton diary entry. Diary entries were sporadic for several months, thus this entry is not dated. Roxton marriage conducted in February 1746, so this entry made in February 1776.]

Our thirtieth wedding anniversary

Today is our 30th wedding anniversary and it only seems it was yesterday I first spied you fencing in the Princes Courtyard at Versailles, stripped to your shirtsleeves, which was most scandalous indeed. Oh, but I could not take my eyes off you and I knew then, as the sun rises each morning, that we were meant to be together for the rest of our lives. Yes, you smile and nod your agreement, but there was a time when you were as skeptical as everyone else, but I will not hold that against you! Have I not always said that one must listen to the heart? It is a most determined organ, and where love is concerned the heart will win out every time against the mind. The arguments of others mean nothing, for was it not Boileau who said that the proof of the pudding is in the eating? And what a most wondrously tasty pudding our marriage it makes!

I had my ladies lay out the gown *a la Turque* that you like me in best, in the soft shell pink silk embroidered in gold thread, and with the matching silk slippers that have the little gold tassels. I wore it to the Ottoman Ambassador's ball and you said you feared I might be snatched away for his harem, and that perhaps you would forbid me wearing such a fetching outfit in public. I pretended to be cross that you had discovered my plan to infiltrate the Ambassador's harem and learn what the women they do there all day locked away from male company. I remember also at the ball you dared to direct your quizzing glass at the Ambassador when he was enquiring of me about our visit to Constantinople.

You stared His Excellency up and down as if the poor man did indeed wish to kidnap me! I had to stop myself from giggling because he became very nervous to be so inspected through your magnified eye, and his forehead it began to bead with sweat. But that could also have been a circumstance of his heavy silk turban that Vallentine said made the Ambassador look like a loaf of bread with an overlarge crust. I still do not understand how people they are so intimidated by you, when me I see that you are one big tease, and I just want to giggle behind my fan! I think you, M'sieur le Duc, missed your calling, and should have been upon the stage. Though, you have always commanded an audience without the need for a theater to stage your performance, have you not?

Julian and Deb's little ones are thriving. I have been to visit the big house once or twice this last month, and to hear their laughter as they race around the garden is a joy. Yes, I know I should visit more often, but Julian he does not like them chattering away in French with this silly morose creature who once was their grandmother. He wants them to grow up English children and so they are to speak that language first, and not their grandparents' first language. I know you agree with him, so it is no use me arguing the point with you, or him.

Oh, I nearly forgot to mention that in honor of our anniversary, just three days ago Cornelia presented Scipio with a second litter of pups. Three fawn-and-white bitches and two black-and-tan dogs, all healthy. I promised one to Martin as a companion for his Delilah, who has turned nine and is looking frail. I think a pup will put the wag back in her tail, and also give Martin something, or should I say someone, to focus on other than worrying about me. To own a truth, I have been a big coward with Martin and cannot bear to face him since you went away without me.

Why? Why did you leave me like this? Why am I here in this house alone? I exist, but I am not here, am I? I eat without tasting. I drink without knowing I am thirsty. I fall asleep hoping the day it is but a dream. I hope against hope that when I lay my head upon the pillow, I will wake from this nightmare and you will be there asleep beside me, and I will tell you my silly fears, and you will take me in your arms and kiss them away. My head hurts, and my heart it aches so much it is like I am carrying a big heavy weight in my chest, and I do not care anymore if my heart it stops. I stare out the window at the lake and I think today is the day I will walk down to the jetty, and keep on walking, through the reeds and out into the middle of the water, my petticoats heavy with water with every dragging step until I am no longer able to move my legs, and the water it is up to my chin and then I will close my eyes and open my mouth and the water it will rush in—

I went away and washed my face and Michelle made me a cup of coffee, so now I am more myself. I read the last paragraph, and I am sorry. All of it is true, of course, but I ask your forgiveness for being so morbid on this of all days. I will try and not be so stupidly selfish and say such

ridiculous things, because I know it upsets you and
Vallentine and Estée to see me not being myself. Have I
told you all how very pleased I am the three of you are
together again? But of course, that too makes me sad
because you are together without me!

It is as well I have my visit to the mausoleum to look
forward to. I will bring Scipio with me, so you can see
how well your boy is doing, and what a proud sire he is.
Of course, when the puppies they are bigger I shall bring
them for your inspection, and you can watch them run
about and we can decide together which one Martin
should have.

Happy anniversary, my darling.

Her Grace the Most Noble Duchess of Roxton, Treat via Alston, Hampshire, to The Right Honorable Lady Mary Cavendish, Abbey Wood via Bisley, Gloucestershire.

Treat via Alston, Hampshire
May, 1776

Dearest Mary, your letter offering your condolences on the loss Julian and I recently suffered had me shedding a tear. You are right, of course, and we do count our blessings in having four happy, healthy children. I suppose it was doubly sad that it happened when it did, because it is my first miscarriage, and also because the news of a new baby lifted everyone's spirits, which as you know have been very low since M'sieur le Duc's passing two years ago.

That sad event is as if it happened yesterday, and Julian has moments where he is walking about in a fog of grief. Thank God for the children, who keep him—no, both of us—grounded and occupied, and stop us from descending into a blue melancholy such as that suffered by his mother. We are determined to be as happy as we can be, for them, and they keep us looking forward not backwards.

Little Juliana was only just born, as you remember, and not a month old when M'sieur le Duc died. Louis and Gus have no recollection of him either. Saddest of all is my Frederick, who tells me about sitting on his Grand-pere's silken knee to be read to, and to listen to his stories of the old King of France. But what is so much worse for Frederick is his Grandmere's sorry state, which has made him a very confused little boy. She is nothing like the grandmother he remembers, and I know it troubles him, though he is only just turned six. He has an old head on his shoulders, which is a great pity for him.

I still have moments where I am truly amazed at the enor-mous influence my father-in-law had on all who came within his orbit, not least his family. You know this as well as anyone, Mary, having grown up with him since your birth. Indeed, your loving recollection of him teaching you to play at backgammon when you were twelve years old, and had lost your own father in traumatic circum-stances, brought tears to my eyes. You wrote about him with such affection that had I not been privileged to know him as my father-in-law for the few short years that I did, I would hardly think it possible you were writing about the same nobleman who had a very different public face to the one he showed his family.

While I was never completely comfortable in his company at any time, I was able to relax a little when all the family was gathered, for I could see in their manner and conver-sation that they loved him unconditionally. His family was everything to him. He adored them, and they adored him.

What I find fascinating is that for all intents and purposes, my father-in-law was the embodiment of the arrogant nobleman. Disdainful of those beneath him whom he deemed inferior of character, he always carried an air of expectation that when he spoke, all should listen, and that his word was law. He did this with his family too, and there were times when he could make me shiver with dread, particularly when he directed his gaze and had that way of looking right through you, as if your words, indeed your very presence, were of no interest to him. Thankfully, I was never on the receiving end of such a look. He was very economical with his words, as if speaking more than was necessary was an effort he did not need to exert. Of course, such silences were always filled by Maman-Duchess, and he was most happy when she did so.

Thank you for extending your kind invitation for Maman-Duchess to visit you, but the truth is, she is not fit company for anyone, and is best left to her inconsolable grief at the Dower House. Julian visits her when he can, but admits to me that he wonders why he does so, because she hardly sees him and barely says two words.

Please keep all this to yourself, dear Mary, for Julian would not thank me for breaking his confidence, but I need to confide in someone in the family or I would surely go mad myself! So, please, I beg of you, lock my letters away, and one day, when I ask it of you, burn them all.

What I am about to tell you, I have told no other.

Julian has called in a physician who specializes in broken minds, to assess and treat his mother. He thinks we should have engaged his services much earlier than this, when her strange habits were first reported. Mary, please, you must say nothing of this. But believe me when I tell you that Maman-Duchess has taken to conversing with the carved marble likeness atop M'sieur le Duc's tomb. She visits the mausoleum daily, taking flowers and books, and sits there all day, talking to the old Duke as if he were still alive and he answering her chatter.

I have not seen this alarming behavior for myself, nor has Julian, but it has been reported by various sources, so it must be true. What first alerted Julian to the possibility his mother refused to believe her husband was truly dead, is that she never refers to M'sieur le Duc, or as she sometimes calls him, Monseigneur, in the past tense. She speaks as if he is still very much alive. Indeed she does the same when referring to Lord and Lady Vallentine. I hardly know what to say in reply, and when she makes a remark about telling M'sieur le Duc about this and that when she returns home, it takes all my self-control to remain insensible.

It breaks my heart and alarms me, because it has pushed Julian to this breaking point of calling in a medical professional. I only hope he is able to help her before it is too late and she needs to be shut away for good. That unthinkable action has never been raised between Julian and me, so again, please, this must remain between the two of us.

Of course, our other worry now is Henri-Antoine, who is utterly neglected by his grieving mother so that it might as well be as if he has lost both his parents, not just his father. It astounds me to think here is a mother who monitored her son's every waking moment from birth to the age of twelve, consumed with worry about the seizures he suffered as a result of the falling sickness, and the instant M'sieur le Duc dies, it is as if her interest in her youngest son also died that day. For she has not asked after him, been near him, sent for Dr. Bailey to ask after his health, or even asked Julian or me how he fares. For all she cares—and I am being very cruel here, but I am angry —he could have died from one of these seizures and such a tragedy would not register with her.

How can she be so unfeeling within the blink of an eye? What must that poor boy be thinking, to have lost his father and his mother, who doted upon him every single day of his life? Of course, the burden for his care now falls to Julian. Not that he, or we, see it as a burden, we love Harry (as we prefer to call him) as much as we love our own children, but I do worry about the state of his young mind. Thank God his seizures have not been so severe of late, or as frequent, and thank God he has Jack!

Good dependable Jack, who watches over Harry and loves him as a brother. Still, Julian frets as to the future, but it quiets his heart to know the boys are enjoying their time at Eton, despite Bailey being just one step behind. Though I think the brothers have struck up some agreement where the future of the good doctor is concerned, as Harry and Jack went off to school in a much better frame of mind, and with a conspiratorial nod to the Duke they possibly hoped I did not catch! I mean to find out what precisely is going on there, when I have a moment to spare.

You will think seriously about my offer for you and Teddy to come stay with us for a month when it pleases you, won't you? I know I don't paint a very rosy picture of life here at Treat, but it is much better to be here than to read about it in one of my depressing missives.

I am fully sensible that it is now a year since Gerald's passing, and so you must be out of your mourning, or nearly so. With the estate in the capable hands of its steward, and Julian well pleased with Mr. Bryce's capabilities in that quarter, you can afford to leave Abbey Wood and visit us. Surely Mr. Bryce will give his permission for Teddy to visit her cousins. As for Teddy, she must sorely be in need of company and new surroundings, as much as her mamma. So please, do give our offer serious consideration, and apply to Mr. Bryce at once. He cannot be so hard-hearted as to deny you, which, if he denies Teddy leaving Abbey Wood, is denying you, for I know you will not leave without her!

The children keep us focused on what is important, and they do lift our spirits so that we can go whole days without reference to the past, and your coming to stay would only increase this happy time. It would be particularly beneficial for Teddy to be around her young cousins, and I am sure she would love to mother Juliana, who is quite the princess, in every respect.

I hear the children returned to the garden after being down at the lake sailing their toy boats, and I will sign off so this letter can be sealed and sent with the Duke's post this afternoon. If I have more to write, it will come in the next post, a sennight after you receive this.

I expect to read of your date of arrival in your next post.

All our love,
Deborah

*Mr. Christopher Bryce, c/o Abbey Wood via Bisley, Glouces-
tershire, to His Grace The Most Noble Duke of Roxton, Treat
via Alston, Hampshire.*

c/o Abbey Wood via Bisley, Gloucestershire
August, 1776

My Lord Duke,

I trust this letter finds you and your family in excellent
health.

As I am not one for unimportant conversation, and I have
no wish to use up ink in wasting your valuable time, I
shall come to the point.

You will find enclosed the usual report, entrusted as it
always is to your secretary Mr. Audley, for delivery to Your
Grace. I trust you will find everything in it satisfactory, as
Mr. Audley did himself when he settled himself in to
peruse the account books and correspondence therein to
do with this estate.

I have no objection to reporting matters to Your Grace,

for that was one of the terms of Sir Gerald's will. We are both bound as co-executors of that document, and I more so as steward of the estate until Sir John reaches his majority, and also as guardian of my cousin's only child, Theodora. What I continue to object to in the strongest terms is the need for Mr. Audley to come in person all the way into Gloucestershire to view the books on your behalf, when this onerous task could easily be conducted and certified by an appointed intermediary who resides in Circencester or Bath.

It is not for me to wonder how Your Grace is able to carry out daily tasks on your estate without the benefit of Mr. Audley's expertise for seven days out of every quarter.

But what I do wonder is that you must consider my abilities so deficient that you must needs send your secretary, in effect, to look over my shoulder. Or is there perhaps some other underlying purpose as to why Mr. Audley acts as your eyes and ears, which you do not wish to disclose to me? For that, Your Grace, is the only conclusion I can draw after tolerating a year of your secretary's quarterly visits.

You state that matters have not changed since Sir Gerald was alive. That Mr. Audley made regular visits to Abbey Wood on your behalf, and for similar reasons. I concede that when my cousin was alive, he allowed his wants to far exceed his income, and the estate was heavily mortgaged. Thus Sir Gerald was forced to acquiesce to your demands to have his affairs overseen, or run the very real risk of having Your Grace call in the substantial loans you made him to keep the estate a viable concern. Since my cousin's untimely death and my subsequent stewardship, there has been a marked improvement in the estate, so much so that a third of the debt is already paid. So, I ask you again, Duke, why the need for Mr. Audley to continue with his visits? They are not needed and they are certainly not wanted.

To be blunt, I do not like the man. His presence disrupts the daily routine, not only of the estate, but of the household. Lady Mary is obliged to treat him as a guest, and I am obligated to allow her to do so. He acts above his station, and because he is here on your business, he acts as if he himself is a duke come amongst us. Though I confess to never having met a duke, so would not know one if I fell over one. I mean you no disrespect, Your Grace, but I am for plain speech, and as co-executors, I will treat you as my equal, with politeness and verisimilitude, nothing more, and nothing less.

You have raised again the matter of the guardianship of Sir Gerald's only child, and that you and your dear duchess have Lady Mary's blessing for Theodora to be reared at your estate with your own children. You feel, and let me quote from your letter, 'Theodora would have the upbringing she deserves amongst her own kin, and want for nothing as my ward'.

That is all well and good for you to wish it, but it was not what Sir Gerald wanted. In fact, you know as well as I that my cousin's will stated that he expressly forbade his only child from being brought up amongst his wife's relatives. He did not state why, but he was emphatic in this matter, and while I could speculate as to his reasons, I will not, nor should you. I cannot account for the working of Sir Gerald's mind in appointing a man who has never married, and who is childless, as the best guardian for an eight-year-old child, a girl child at that. Sir Gerald entrusted his daughter to my care until she married or turned five-and-twenty, whichever was the sooner, and thus I will do my duty by her and him. It would be best for all concerned, but most of all for Theodora, if this matter were now let to drop altogether. I will not change my mind in this, and Lady Mary knows I will not.

In respect of Theodora's future, I request—no, I demand, as is my right as her guardian—that you refrain from further overtures to Lady Mary in seeking her blessing to remove the child from my care. Not only is gaining such a blessing worthless because I am intractable on the matter, but by approaching Lady Mary you have no doubt caused her unnecessary anxiety. Naturally, she would wish to acquiesce to your request—I doubt anyone has refused you—but she knows my thoughts, and thus she must naturally be torn between your demands and my intractability. For her to give you her blessing as to her daughter's care can only be wasted wishful thinking.

In that same letter you were candid enough with me to publicly voice your concerns for the welfare and well-being of the Lady Mary. Let me do you the same courtesy. As Lady Mary is Theodora's mother, and for as long as the child needs her mother, Lady Mary may continue to consider Abbey Wood her home. As such, she will be accorded every courtesy in that capacity and not, as I am sure you would prefer me to do, because she is the daughter of an earl and cousin of a ducal house. I am well aware Sir Gerald was one for preening for his wife's titled relatives, and spreading his conversation with lashings of his noble connections, but under my stewardship Abbey Wood is a working farm. As such there is no room, and I do not have the time, to indulge such artifice.

And on the subject of Lady Mary and your generous proposal to supplement her allowance so that it is commensurate with her birthright, again I decline on her behalf. Please do not put the offer to me again for I will again refuse you, which will, no doubt, become something of an embarrassment to a nobleman such as yourself who expects unquestioning obedience. And just so you are aware, I have made it plain to Lady Mary that if she were to accept such an allowance from you, she may also take up your offer to reside with you and your good duchess, but her daughter remains here with me.

I neither seek or want your good opinion, Your Grace. Nor do I need your patronage. I am a free agent and intend to remain that way. That does not mean we cannot be civil to one another and strive for the same goals. I have two: That Theodora grows into a well-mannered, happy young woman; and that the heir to Abbey Wood, Sir John Cavendish, inherits a property upon his twenty-first birthday that is worthy of his birthright and allows him to live as a gentleman. I am certain Your Grace wishes for nothing less.

I remain Your Grace's humble servant,
Christopher Bryce, Esq.

The Honorable Charles Fitzstuart, St. James's Mews, Westminster, London, to The Right Honorable Major Lord Fitzstuart, Fitzstuart Hall via Denham, Buckinghamshire.

St. James's Mews, Westminster
May 1777

Dearest brother, by the time you read this I will have absconded to France with Sarah-Jane Strang. Eloped more belike, though I hope to seek her father's blessing for our elopement before we leave. You are not at all surprised, are you? I can hear your loud laugh from here, Dair! You are shaking your head and wondering why it took me this long to get up the courage to do both.

You knew long ago, did you not, that my political leanings and my conscience were all for the rebel cause in the colonies, and yet you never said a word against me. Indeed you could have turned me in to Shrewsbury as a spy and a traitor, and you did not! That you never once quizzed me, I am a thousand times grateful.

You who are fiercely loyal to king and country, who risked life and limb a hundred times over for both, who has led men into battle (a bloody business)—and I have heard

Mr. Farrier tell of some of your shared exploits—you are a hero to so many, and to me, your little brother. But what must you think me but a traitorous dog, and I do not blame you.

Whatever your thoughts of me, you must know I will always love and admire you most sincerely and devotedly. No one could ask for a better, a more honorable big brother. And I will be the first to raise a glass in a toast when you finally inherit the earldom, which is nothing less than you deserve. I don't care what others think of you, that they call you an arrogant blusterer and a care-for-nobody, or that my republican sensibilities cannot be reconciled to your monarchist principles, you are my flesh and blood, you are my brother, and my heart knows you for a good and decent man. I am proud to tell anyone who asks that my big brother is a noble man, not only by birth, but by word and deed.

And did you not do me a good deed by giving me the shove I needed to declare myself to Miss Strang? When did you suspect I had fallen in love with my dear heart? You have such a wider experience of women, and you know your little brother well, that I am sure it did not take you many minutes in our company to discover my feelings for her!

I confess to you now, and hang my head in shame that I was in an agony that you had your eye on Miss Strang, for her considerable inheritance. Now I realize you were being my big brother and trying to ascertain if her feelings for me were genuine and reciprocated! Sarah-Jane has told me so, and was not a little indignant that you suspected her for a fickle female! But she has forgiven you and begs yours in return.

We plan to settle in the town of Versailles, and I will take up the post of interpreter and translator to Mr. Benjamin

Franklin. An honor indeed, which Cousin Duchess will confirm, as she has the highest opinion of Mr. Franklin's mind, if not his politics! I hope one day to make you as proud of me as I am of you, dearest brother. I mean to strive every day in this endeavor.

Please give my love to Mother and to Mary. I suspect you are grinding your teeth at the prospect of having to explain my behavior to Mother, but perhaps it will be her melodramatic reaction to the news I am marrying the daughter of a nabob that will be more devastating and send her into sobs, prostrate on her couch. Yes, I am heavily in your debt.

Keep an eye on Mary, and her situation. She is a widow now, and well rid of her pompous husband, who was beneath her in character and situation—I know, I have bravely written in ink what we both thought of that match, but neither of us was of an age or in a situation to do anything about it at the time, were we? Now, at least you can. Again, it is all left on your shoulders, which are wide enough to carry the burden of family.

I wrote to Father with my news. I know that means less than nothing to you, but it is a courtesy I felt beholden to undertake. Look upon it as one you now do not need to perform. Thus I have saved you the obligation!

Write when and if you can. I will miss you.

Until we meet again, and we will.

Your loving brother,
Charlie

Mr. Jonathon Strang Leven, c/o Lawson and Gower Chambers, Gray's Inn Road, London, to the Honorable Mrs. Charles Fitzstuart, c/o The Honorable Charles Fitzstuart, 21 Rue du Peintre Lebrun, Versailles, France.

c/o Lawson and Gower Chambers, Gray's Inn Road,
London
May 1777

Dearest Sarah-Jane, I am leaving these few pages with Mme la Duchesse to be posted upon my departure for Scotland. I did not want this letter to perhaps overtake you, and to arrive before you had time to settle in your new home in Versailles, and in your new role as wife.

I know you and Charles will be happy together. He is a good man and will be the best of husbands. Your most difficult task as a wife will be to rally him from a deep-seated seriousness, so that upon occasion he can find the laughter in life, and perhaps enjoy the moment for its own sake, rather than always considering the grand scheme of things. But, he will tell you so himself, he is changing history, and for the better of the majority. He will be caught up in many a political machination as secretary and interpreter to Mr. Franklin. I do not envy the heavy burden of responsibility that will be placed upon his young shoulders to put Mr. Franklin's arguments to His French Majesty as to why he should support the rebels, for it will bring with it war with England. And war is never a good thing, for either side.

I have told you often enough but I shall ink it down again, how very proud I am of you, as my daughter and as a female in your own right. I am proud of myself, too, in how well I have raised you, for your mother would surely be proud of me! Your papa is ever the tease, is he not, my darling girl?

Let me be serious a little longer, and tell you that tonight I go to the theater in company with Mme la Duchesse, and so by tomorrow morning, the news will be all over town that we are lovers, and it is the truth. You know it is so, and possibly she told you so herself when you had your private interview before your departure. She is ever truthful. Thus you cannot be shocked to see it written here. But we are more than lovers, much more. We are soul mates. I believe this with my whole heart.

I am in love with Antonia Roxton and have been since I first set eyes on her. Something happened to me that night of the Roxton Easter Ball that I cannot explain. I just knew from that moment forward I had to be with her, would die for her if need be, that she is the only woman with whom I want to spend the rest of my life. I tried to tell you this upon numerous occasions, and at first you would not listen to your Papa. I tried to understand why you could not, and reasoned to myself that your youth and inexperience must account for it, but also perhaps you were a little jealous your Papa is so in love?

Now you are married and your eyes opened to love in all

its forms, and you are loved in return, you see that it is impossible to understand the heart as one does the mind. Thus it is best to let the heart have its way without argument. I know it worries you that I am in love with a woman who is a decade older than I. But our ages are nothing but numbers. How old we are is more about how we act, how we see, and what we feel. If you were to use your mind and not your heart to assess the man you love and have married, you would surely see him differently, perhaps as others here see him—a man who committed treason by trading secrets with the rebels about the British war effort in the colonies. Yet, this is not how your heart sees him. Your heart tells you here is a man of conviction and purpose, who believes in a higher calling, who is doing what he believes is right and just for the future of the American colonies, and thus he has your respect and your love. And he loves you.

Antonia Roxton loves me. I am as sure of this as I am that the sky is blue and the grass is green. I mean to marry her before I head north. I am also utterly convinced that our marriage will be blessed with children. So you are no longer to worry about your Papa, for he will never be lonely again. And you certainly can be very happy that he rides north to fulfill his destiny. Most reluctantly, as you know, but fulfill it I must. You may have married a republican, but that should not make you any less proud your papa has ascended to a Scottish dukedom.

And so, my fair cherub, this will be the last letter I write under my own name, and from London. I will send you tidings from north of the border, when I arrive in Edinburgh. From there you will receive a letter from His Grace the Most Noble Duke of Kinross, sealed with the ducal coat of arms. Do not hide your joy from Charles. If I know anything of that young man, he will be as pleased as you to know his father-in-law is safe and well. And of course he will be overjoyed when you tell him his cousin is now the Duchess of Kinross, and in truth his mother-in-law. Ah, the complicated lives we lead!

Do your Papa the favor of writing to my new duchess and bestow your blessing upon our marriage. I have convinced her that in time you will come to love her, and yet who can blame her for her apprehension, particularly as she is fully sensible to how much I love you and value your good opinion? I know Charles will do so, but her mind will not be easy until she sees your blessing in your own hand, whatever Charles may write on your behalf. Here are my thanks in advance, sealed with a kiss.

I look forward to hearing all your news, and how your French language classes are progressing. I trust Mrs. Spencer is proving her worth as your companion, and you are both enjoying the lovely Spring weather. Pass on my regards to my son-in-law, and if Charles would like to write to me, I would be honored.

It is time for me to dress for the theater and there meet my future relations, my other son-in-law, to be precise! His Grace of Roxton has a box, and your Papa cannot wait to see that nobleman's features as I take my place beside his divine mamma. I predict poor Dick Sheridan's new play will then become a mere sideshow to unfolding events amongst the noble audience. Yes, that is the sound of your naughty papa rubbing his hands together with glee! Until Scotland.

> Love and best,
> Your loving Papa
> J S L

[Antonia Roxton diary entry.]

Friday May 9, 1777

<u>The morning after opening night of Sheridan's *School for Scandal*</u>

Renard, I saw the most wonderful play last night. School for Scandal by Richard Sheridan. I predict it will be enduring, it is very witty. I told you all about it upon one of my visits before coming up to London. I was in two minds whether to attend the performance, because I have not been to the theater without you. But Jonathon he convinced me, and I did so very much want to see if the actors could do Sheridan's writing justice. Of course, there was too much noise and chatter, and the eyes of many upon me, but I tried not to let that worry me, as you were used to doing. My fan helped, but I own your quizzing glass is a much better weapon of choice to quell the masses upon such public occasions.

Julian he was there with Deb, and Martin came along, too. The boys sat with us, and at interval, Julian came across to our box with Martin on his arm. Martin was leaning more heavily than usual on his stick because he had a fall while alighting from his carriage. It is nothing for you to worry about and the bruise will heal in no time.

Oh, but Renard, I wish you could have seen Julian's face when I introduced Martin to Jonathon! Jonathon shook Martin's hand heartily, as if they were old friends, then remarked it was good to finally meet the other man in Antonia's life! Oh yes! That is what Jonathon he said! Can you believe it? *Incroyable* is it not? I gave a gasp and then rapped him upon the knuckles for his impertinence. And what did he do? He laughed and snatched the fan from me and playfully chucked me under the chin. And all this before two hundred pairs of eyes. Poor Julian could hardly breathe from the embarrassment. Martin was transfixed, and because he spent so many years with you, he did what you always do in such socially awkward situations, he said nothing. Nothing! But me I am attuned to both of you, and know you let your eyes do the talking for you. And this is what Martin did. So I saw the gleam in his eye and the smile, too. He even dared to actually smile when he turned away to speak to Henri-Antoine. Poor Julian did not know where to look or what to say to such outlandish behavior. I felt a little sorry for him, because it must be so awkward for him to be in the presence of his mother's lover, particularly when this man is not much older than he. It helped to break the tension, I think, when he was told Deborah was waving at us from their box, and he turned and relaxed a little. And then it was time for the interval to be over, so they returned to their seats.

Martin is staying with Julian and Deborah, and they will all join us this morning for the ceremony. I am so very pleased he is here for that. It will help Julian get through it, and feel he has at least one ally in the room, for Deborah, she, too, approves of Jonathan, as does everyone else.

Henri-Antoine and Jack are staying with me for a week after the ceremony, and then they are returning to Oxford and their studies. They have promised me, and I will hold them to their word. Henri-Antoine he is very intelligent but tries to hide it, I think for Jack's sake. Not that Jack is unintelligent. But in Henri-Antoine there is a quickness of brain and understanding that is rare in one of his age. He is also an excellent linguist, like you, and can switch between English and French without hesitation. He listens to Jonathan in English, and to me in French, and answers us in our respective languages. It is most extraordinary, but we do not do it often, because Jack he is not so linguistically gifted. But then, who is?

I always knew our son was the image of you, did I not tell you so? And as he grows older and becomes more a man, the more apparent this likeness becomes, which should please you. I cannot lie that it does not sometimes give me a pain in the heart to see him and to hear him. More than once I have turned at his voice and expected you, my love, to be standing there. Our younger son he even sits in the manner you do, silent and observant, always assessing any given situation before speaking when in public. And just like you, when he is behind closed doors with those he truly loves and thus is completely comfortable, he transforms and is relaxed and smiling. He loves games of charades and has an infectious laugh—which I might add are the only attributes he seems to have inherited from his mamma! Oh, and perhaps his love of reading, too—it is as if it is you come amongst us again… To hear him laugh again! It truly is music to my ears. And he is happy—I think because his mamma she has finally returned to the land of the living, and to him. I have missed him so much, and he, me.

But I have not told you the most startling piece of news of all! Our son's episodes of falling sickness have abated to the point that Bailey he is no longer his shadow, and has not been these past two years. I can hardly believe it myself, Renard, but Henri-Antoine assures me it is so, and that the last episode he suffered was some twelve months ago, and it was only a mild one at that. This makes me so very happy, and I wanted to hug my little boy and kiss him and cry all at the same time. Of course I did not do this, for what boy who is about to turn sixteen wants his mamma acting like a madwoman before his best friend? Though I think Jack he would not have minded in the least. So now you can stop worrying and perhaps I will, too. Though I still cannot believe the sickness has truly left him. But Jonathon says Jack will always watch Henri-Antoine's back, and so we will leave it to him to tell us if there is any change.

I will confess it because I know you will not mind in the least, and even Julian he is pleased by it too, Henri-Antoine truly likes Jonathon, and Jonathon him. It is a lovely sight to see them in each other's company, relaxed and talking as if they have known each other since Henri-Antoine was a small boy. But I think that is Jonathon's gift, to put people at their ease with his agreeable charm. Just like Vallentine was used to doing, if Vallentine was slightly more vague in his delivery. How I miss my friend. But he is with you and Madam, and so I am a little jealous the three of you have each other, and left me here alone. And because I have been so very alone— no! That is now not true. But I did not take this man as my lover to simply end my loneliness but because I love him. I love him, Renard, and I did not think it at all possible that I would ever feel this way again with another man but you. But I cannot lie to my own heart, now can I? Or to you. There I have confessed all, and written it here in ink in my diary, and I will tell you to your face when next I visit you. But you did urge me to live and love again, and while I never believed it possible, it has happened without any will or seeking on my part.

Oh! Please excuse me for not telling you earlier. I have accepted Jonathon's offer of marriage; the man has asked me so many times I have lost count. He truly does love me, even though he knows that in marrying me, he must forever share me with you. *Mon Dieu*, I have just read back that sentence and it sounds very naughty indeed. Ha! Let it stay that way, for it is true. Jonathon must share me with you, for I am not whole without you.

This is what you wanted for me all along, is it not, my love? And me I would not listen—I could not, then. I could not contemplate a life without you, and to own a truth there are moments when I am still dazed to think you will not walk through a doorway and join me. But as I live and breathe, I know I must do more than just exist. For how can I face you one day to hear you scold me for wasting what life was left to me? When the day comes for us to be reunited forever, it will be such a joyous occasion and I will embrace it wholeheartedly, but for now I am here, and this morning I am getting married and begin a new chapter in my life.

So I sign this letter for you, my darling love, as the Duchess of Roxton, but for the last time until I am reunited with you. Until then it will be as the Duchess of Kinross that I next sit before you, and I know that will please you very much.

Au revoir, my love,
Antonia, Duchess of Roxton

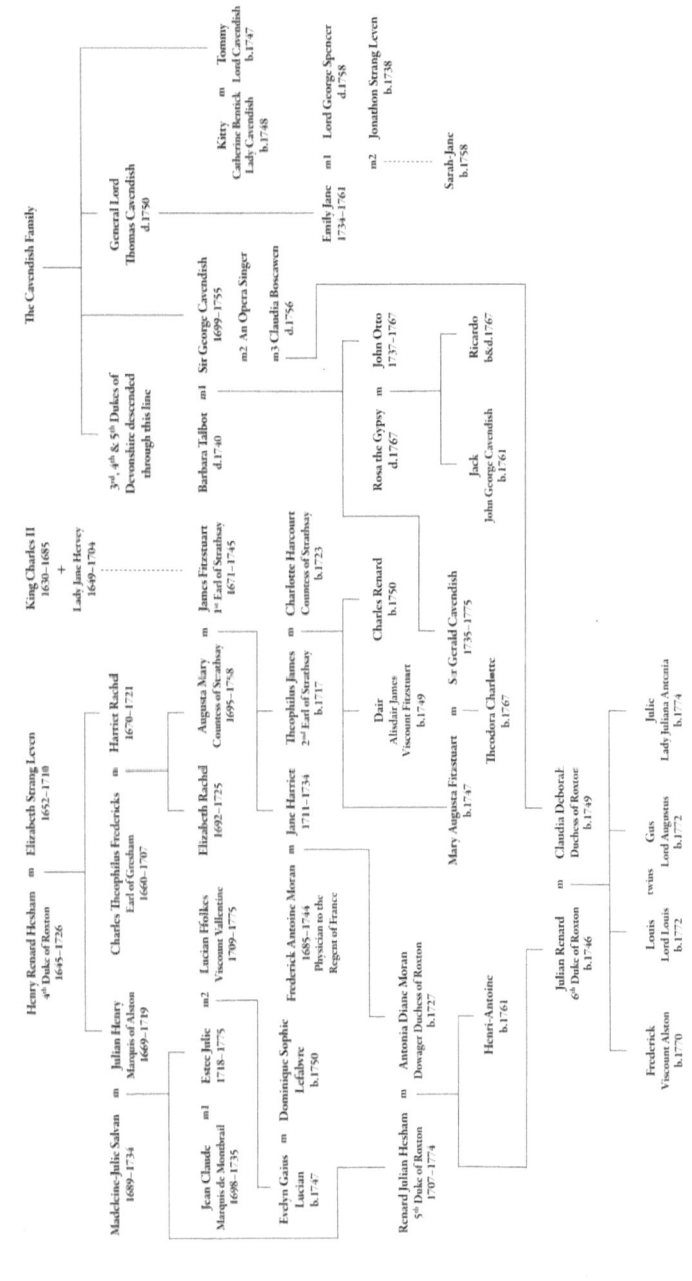

The Cavendish Family

General Lord
Thomas Cavendish
d.1750

Kitty   m   Tommy
Catherine Renwick   Lord Cavendish
Lady Cavendish   b.1747
b.1748

Emily Jane   m1   Lord George Spencer
1734-1761   d.1757

m2   Jonathon Strang Leven
b.1758

Sarah Jane
b.1758

3rd, 4th & 5th Dukes of
Devonshire descended
through this line

Sir George Cavendish
1699-1755
m2. An Opera Singer
m3 Claudia Boscawen
d.1756

Barbara Talbot   m1
d.1740

John Otto   m   Rosa the Gypsy
1737-1767   d.1767

Ricardo
bkd.1767

Jack
John George Cavendish
b.1761

King Charles II
1630-1685
+
Lady Jane Hervey
1649-1704

Henry Renard Hesham   m   Elizabeth Strang Leven
4th Duke of Roxton   1652-1710
1645-1726

Charles Theophilus Fredericks   m   Harriet Rachel
Earl of Gersham   1670-1721
1660-1707

Augusta Mary   m   James Fitzstuart
Countess of Strathsay   1st Earl of Strathsay
1695-1758   1671-1745

Elizabeth Rachel
1692-1735

Theophilus James   m   Charlotte Harcourt
2nd Earl of Strathsay   Countess of Strathsay
b.1717   b.1723

Jane Harriet
1711-1734

Dair   m   Charles Renard
Alisdair James   b.1750
Viscount Fitzstuart
b.1749

Sr Gerald Cavendish
1735-1775

Mary Augusta Fitzstuart   m   Theodora Charlotte
b.1747   b.1767

Madeleine-Julie Salvan   m   Julian Henry
1689-1734   Marquis of Alston
1669-1719

Estée Julie   m2
1718-1775

Lucian Ffolkes
Viscount Vallentine
1709-1775

Frederick Antoine Moran   m   Jane Harriet
1685-1744   1711-1734
Physician to the
Regent of France

Jean Claude   m1
Marquis de Montbrail
1698-1735

Evelyn Gains   m   Dominique Sophie
Lucian   Lefabvre
b.1747   b.1750

Antonia Diane Moran   m   Renard Julian Hesham
Dowager Duchess of Roxton   5th Duke of Roxton
b.1727   1707-1774

Henri-Antoine
b.1761

Julian Renard   m   Claudia Deborah
6th Duke of Roxton   Duchess of Roxton
b.1746   b.1749

Frederick
Viscount Alston
b.1770

Louis
Lord Louis
b.1772

Louis   twins   Gus
Lord Louis   Lord Augustus
b.1772   b.1772

Julie
Lady Juliana Antonia
b.1774

BEHIND-THE-SCENES

Explore the places, objects, and history in
Eternally Yours on Pinterest.

www.pinterest.com/lucindabrant